A
DANGEROUS TIDE

Kristi Holl

Annie's®
AnniesFiction.com

Books in the Secrets of the Quilt series

Library of Congress-in-Publication Data
A Dangerous Tide / by Kristi Holl
p. cm.
I. Title
                    2015947210

AnniesFiction.com
(800) 282-6643
Secrets of the Quilt™
Series Creator: Shari Lohner
Series Editors: Shari Lohner, Janice Tate, and Ken Tate
Cover Illustrator: Jonathan Bouw

10 11 12 13 14 | Printed in China | 9 8 7 6 5

1

Cabot Falls, Vermont
Present Day

*R*elax, Sofia Parker told herself firmly. *It's Sunday, a peaceful, restful day.* She took a couple of deep breaths.

"Vanessa, Wynter, come on," she called upstairs. "We'll be late for church if we don't leave now." Jim and the boys had gone early to help set up a sound system for the small orchestra playing that morning.

Waiting at the front door, Sofia turned sideways before the hall mirror. Did her dress show her recent five-pound gain? Sighing, she dug through her purse for her keys, then remembered that Vanessa had borrowed them on Saturday.

Wynter came downstairs first, dressed in cords and a sweater warm enough for Vermont's late winter. Behind her, Vanessa looked chilly in her flared skirt and striped blouse. Sofia smiled and held out her hand. "I need my keys, and you'll need a coat this morning."

Vanessa frowned. "Didn't I put your keys back in your purse?"

"I can't find them."

Blond hair falling over her face, Vanessa searched her own purse, then her jacket pockets. "I don't have them."

"Vanessa! Not again." Sofia lowered her volume. "Run upstairs and check the jeans you wore yesterday. And hurry."

"Can't we just use the spare key under the bumper?"

"We could," Sofia said, "but then we wouldn't have my house keys, and I want to lock up."

The year before, right after Vanessa got her license, she had left the keys locked in the Suburban with the engine running. For future emergencies, Jim stuck a magnetic box containing a spare key under the back bumper.

"Wait." Wynter disappeared into the kitchen for a moment and then reappeared, dangling the lost keys. "In the tea basket," she said, rolling her eyes. She jammed a knit cap down over her long black hair.

Wynter was much easier to understand these days, thanks to her speech therapy. Being able to hear after receiving her cochlear implant was making such a difference in her life. Sofia knew she still had some work to do to catch up—including personal tutoring—but at fifteen, she had an excellent chance of graduating with her class in a few years.

Sofia set the house alarm and locked the door leading to the garage. When she slid behind the wheel of the car, Vanessa was already on her phone in the backseat.

"No problem. It's all worked out," she said. Then she slipped her phone into her purse.

"Who're you calling on a Sunday morning?" Sofia asked as she was backing out.

"Just Abby," Vanessa said.

"What's 'all worked out'?"

Silence. Sofia glanced at Vanessa in the rearview mirror. "Vanessa?"

"How I'm getting our joint science project to school tomorrow," she said. "Remember, you said I could take your car and go early to set it up in the gym."

Sofia turned onto Main Street and drove past the covered walking bridge, enjoying the light Sunday-morning traffic. "Just don't lose my keys again."

"I keep telling you I need keys of my own. A car of my own would be even better."

Wynter leaned forward and touched Sofia's shoulder. "Do I have to go in early too?"

"No, she's not," Vanessa snapped.

"Like who wants to?" Wynter said. "Mom?"

"No, Wynter, you and the boys can go with Dad." Jim taught math at the high school, and he'd drop Luke and Matthew off at the middle school on the way.

Sofia continued past the downtown square with its art galleries, crafts shops, restaurants, and the century-old inn. Their church, with the tall white steeple, was at the end of the road. Getting out of the car, Sofia spotted a book tucked under Vanessa's arm and shook her head. "I love that story, but you're not reading *Pride and Prejudice* during the sermon."

"I'll never finish this book in a week," Vanessa grumbled. "Miss Jameson claims this is great literature, but nothing's happened yet in the first three chapters."

Sofia wisely didn't argue. All through church, her four children were as squirmy as toddlers. The New England snow was finally melting, and spring fever seemed to have hit them all. Jim ran a hand through his thick blond hair and grinned at Sofia over their heads.

Driving home later, Sofia admitted she was restless herself. Part of it was the dissatisfaction with her catering business—what there was of it. She loved creating artistic desserts, but she hadn't had any lucrative catering jobs in weeks.

The other restless urge came from the mystery of the priceless silk patchwork quilt she'd inherited from Nonna, her beloved Italian maternal grandmother who'd helped raise Sofia and her sisters after their mother's death. At a recent family dinner, her older sisters, Gina and Rosa, had probed for a progress report on her quilt research.

Sofia still sensed hard feelings that she, the youngest sister and least accomplished in the sewing arts, should have inherited Nonna's heirloom quilt, which was pieced together from ancient fabrics. Each of twelve different squares in the center was said to be of great historical significance. Sofia had been entrusted with the quest of discovering which distinguished ancestor pieced each square. A leather-bound diary written in Italian accompanied the quilt, and Nonna claimed it contained enough clues to find the answers. She also hinted that Sofia had much more in common with their famous ancestors than she would suspect.

Sofia had read Nonna's letter so many times that she had memorized much of it, especially the promise and the warning. "These prized fabrics," Nonna had written, "have touched the lives of some of the most prominent figures in history—queens, renowned artists, famous musicians, and many more. I daresay the quilt is worth millions, but we will never know for certain as it must never be sold." And then she warned Sofia, "The world can never know the truth about the quilt for it would surely lead to conflict, unspeakable acts of greed . . ."

Sofia had solved the mystery of only two quilt squares so far, but she was eager to start research on the third before spring break, when the kids would commandeer the family computer.

The third square was quite different, an unusual pattern of white embroidery on white silk with a signature in one corner done in light blue. The signature, in English, was most puzzling: "In friendship, J.A." Why were English words in a quilt created by her Italian ancestor?

Hoping for family bonding time after serving them their favorite giant calzone for lunch, Sofia suggested going bowling. Girls against guys was always fun. But Vanessa quashed that idea with her sour announcement that she'd be chained to her chair all day reading *Pride and Prejudice* for her lit class.

"You're so lucky," Sofia said. "That's a classic, one of the great love stories."

"Ugh," Luke and Matthew said together, both reaching for the last piece of spinach-and-sausage calzone. Luke shrugged and let his younger brother have it. At twelve, Luke was peaceable, like his dad, while squirmy ten-year-old Matthew could be a hothead at times.

Jim wrapped his arms around Sofia, and she loved the feel of his worn flannel shirt. "Someday you goons will sing a different tune," he said, kissing the back of her neck.

The boys pretended to gag and took their cupcakes with them down to the family room. "Thirty minutes," Sofia called, "then do something besides video games."

Sofia sighed as she watched her Sunday bonding time with the kids go down the tubes. Wynter cleared the table while Vanessa dramatically laid her head on her folded arms and groaned. Sofia stifled a snicker. Oh, the burdens of being in high school.

"I know," Sofia suddenly said. "Yes yes yes!"

Vanessa sat up, cocked an eyebrow, and waited. Wynter paused in the doorway. Even Jim asked, "What's that light in your eyes?"

"You'll see." She was about to solve Vanessa's problem and make a fabulous bond with her girls. "Vanessa, you need to see the BBC miniseries of *Pride and Prejudice* first. Then you'll speed-read through the book. You won't be able to put it down. I guarantee it."

"Oh Mom, I don't have time."

"Yes, you do," Sofia insisted. "Trust me, after six episodes of Colin Firth as Mr. Darcy, you'll wish there was more."

"I'm outta here," Jim said. "The boys and I will leave you to it."

Sofia tapped her fingers on the table. "Let's see . . . I know. I'll make a real British dessert to eat while we watch. What would put you in the proper mood?"

"Scones?" Wynter asked.

"Mmm, yes, with clotted cream and strawberries," Sofia said.

"Clotted cream?" Vanessa's lip curled. "As in blood clots?"

Sofia laughed. "Clotted cream is superthick, rich cream. It comes from scalding, and it's more like butter than whipped cream." She paged through her cookbook for the recipe. "Actually, it takes an awful lot of cream. Maybe I'll do something else."

After searching several cookbooks, they decided on a traditional British Bakewell tart, a pie-size dessert. "I'll make two of them," Sofia said, "and I can freeze one for my painting group. You can watch the first episode while I bake. That should cover the chapters you've read." She rented the BBC miniseries and turned on the subtitles for Wynter. The British accent would be hard for her to decipher, even with her new implants.

Humming, Sofia gathered ingredients for the Bakewell tart. She rolled out two crusts, then added a layer of raspberry jam to each. After creaming together the butter and sugar, she folded in a mixture of crushed almonds and flour for the next layer.

Occasional comments from the living room made her smile. "Hey, Mom, Colin Firth was a hunk when he was young." *Yup. Just wait until he dives into the pond and later proposes to Elizabeth Bennet.* It was hard for Sofia to believe that this version of *Pride and Prejudice* was more than twenty years old already.

She sprinkled sliced almonds on top and slid both tarts into the oven. By the end of the second episode, the dessert was cool enough to eat. Jim and the boys appeared long enough to get their share, make faces at the movie, and leave again.

After finishing her tart, which practically melted in her mouth, Sofia had as much fun watching Vanessa's and Wynter's reactions as she did watching the show. They were both engrossed, and Vanessa hadn't complained that "nothing happens" since it started.

Sofia reached for a sketch pad tucked down next to her chair. Just for fun, she started sketching caricatures of the characters. By the end of the last episode and the Bennet sisters' double wedding, Sofia had drawn Mrs. Bennet suffering an attack of nerves, Lizzie doing embroidery, Lydia swinging, and Lady Catherine de Bourgh holding court in her drawing room. She couldn't seem to capture Mr. Darcy adequately, though—or maybe she couldn't stand to make him look comical.

"This was a great idea, Mom." Vanessa stood and stretched. "Colin Firth was eye candy back then."

"Jane would call him *amiable*." Sofia winked. "'Beyond a doubt, there cannot be two opinions on that point.' This version follows the book very closely," she added. "You'll recognize the famous speeches."

Vanessa spread Sofia's sketches on the couch. "These are good. Can I take them to lit class tomorrow?"

Sofia was surprised but pleased. "Sure, if you want to."

"It'll be easy since I'll have the car. Remember, I have a prom decoration meeting after school too."

"How will Wynter get home then?"

"I'll wait for her in the library," Wynter said.

"Okay." Sofia handed over the sketches. "Just don't lose my keys this time."

The girls heated some leftovers for supper and then headed upstairs. Sofia sighed. What a perfect Sunday. After six hours of *Pride and Prejudice*, though, it was rather a shock to come back from the 1800s to a kitchen full of dirty dishes.

As Sofia covered the second Bakewell tart with foil, she recalled how the Bennet sisters hurried to look busy embroidering when visitors arrived. She wondered how much of Jane Austen's fabulous stories were autobiographical.

Her hand paused in midair. *Jane Austen. J.A.*

Sofia sat down hard on the kitchen stool, her knees suddenly weak. Embroidery. *"In friendship", J.A. No, it couldn't be.* She was adding two plus two and coming up with ten.

On the other hand, was it possible? Was there even the tiniest chance that Jane Austen, her favorite English novelist, had sewn one of her quilt squares?

Sofia could hardly contain her excitement while she herded all the kids through nighttime routines and into bed. Vanessa didn't even protest going to bed at the same time as Wynter. Snuggled under her quilt, her nose was buried in *Pride and Prejudice* by the time Sofia popped in to say good night to them.

Jim was working at the dining room table when she came back downstairs. "I thought you were done," Sofia said, patting his shoulder.

"Almost." He nodded at his laptop. "Just need to copy the last page of problems for the midterm and check it."

"Okay, I'll see you soon." Upstairs in the master bedroom, Sofia knelt by the carved wooden *cassone* at the foot of the bed. Over five hundred years old, the trunk held her family history. While the diary was written in faded black ink, their true history was recorded in fabric.

Sofia leaned against the trunk and stroked the smooth, soft, leather-covered diary, imagining the generations preceding her who had held it. Nonna had given her an incredible gift and a frightening responsibility. The quilt pieces, some of them hundreds of years old, had been stitched together in the early 1900s, and Sofia's great-great-grandmother had written the diary. For reasons of her own, Nonna had felt Sofia would glean the most from solving the quilt mysteries. She had spoken of strong roots enabling Sofia to spread her branches wide.

"Be all you were created to be," Nonna had told her many times since becoming their "mother" when Sofia was four years old.

Shivering, Sofia pulled an afghan off the bed and tucked it around her shoulders. Trying to keep her expectations in check, she turned the diary's delicate pages until she found *Quadrato Numero Tre,* the third square. She always kept her dual-language dictionary close by, but she found she needed it less and less as she harkened back to her early life being raised by a grandmother whose native tongue was Italian.

As she studied the entry, her hopeful anticipation grew. She knew many of the words. *Bianco* and *lavoro* together meant "whitework." She frowned at *il ricamo,* then remembered it meant "the embroidery." Sofia instantly recalled seeing a white square with white embroidery when she'd studied the quilt. It had been the only square with an edging of lace. She moved her finger down the description. Yes, there it was: *bordo in pizzo.*

She added the words to her notebook, taking meticulous notes. Continuing in the diary, her finger stopped at an English word she knew: *candlewicking.* Sofia wondered why this was in English. A quick check showed her that there was an Italian word for candlewicking, and it meant the same thing. It was a form of whitework embroidery that used unbleached cotton thread on a piece of unbleached muslin. It got its name from the soft spun cotton thread, which was braided and used for wicks in candles.

Candlewicking designs were taken from nature: flowers, trees, butterflies, and birds.

Near the bottom of the entry, other names—English names—jumped out at her. Southampton. England. And 1812. She puzzled over the last phrase—*passeggero clandestino*—and finally had to look it up. Could that be right? "Stowaway"? The *Mediterraneo* was obviously the Mediterranean. But what did "J.A." have to do with it?

Sofia realized that after watching *Pride and Prejudice* all afternoon with the girls, she had Jane Austen on her mind, but could it be true? Could the "J.A." embroidered on the white silk square have been sewn by her favorite author? And what would Southampton have to do with anything? Jane had written her books in Bath and Chawton Village, Sofia already knew, and she was buried in Winchester Cathedral. She'd loved Austen's writings most of her life, and she'd never read anything about her going to Italy, let alone being a stowaway.

Was it even remotely possible that a quilt square made by Jane Austen could end up in Italy to be included in their family heirloom silk quilt? *Well, why not?* Sofia argued with herself. After all, the "In friendship" was in *English*. It didn't say "*in amicizia*."

Monday flew by with laundry for six, cleaning house, and grocery shopping. Sofia was trying something new with the risotto, replacing part of the rice with butternut squash for a beta-carotene boost and more fiber. She wished Jim would get home with the boys soon. He'd taken them to get new shoes for track. She was rinsing her hands when the doorbell rang, followed immediately by two sharp raps on the front door.

Drying her hands on a towel, Sofia hurried to the door to open it. Two police officers stood on her front porch. Her heart skipped a beat, then pounded like fury. *Jim! The boys!* "Yes?"

"May we come in?" one of the officers asked.

Sofia took a closer look at his broad, freckled face. "Ryan?" It *was* Ryan Quimby, a boy from when she went to high school. She didn't know the other officer. "Please. Come in."

"I'm Officer Wood," the second officer said. "Is Vanessa Parker at home?"

"Vanessa?" A flood of relief was followed quickly by curiosity. "Yes." Sofia called her from the living room.

"Vanessa Parker?" the officer asked. When Vanessa nodded, he said, "We need to question you about leaving the scene of an accident this afternoon."

Vanessa stared, mouth open. She licked her lips and cleared her throat. "I don't understand," she said, sounding truly puzzled. "I wasn't in any accident."

"According to witnesses in our report, the car you were driving jumped a curb and drove up onto the sidewalk. There you ran over a tricycle and narrowly missed hitting a child sitting in a wagon."

"No I didn't." Vanessa turned to her mother.

Sofia could barely breathe. "Obviously someone was mistaken in what they thought they saw."

"A witness gave a license plate number and car description of the 2008 Chevy Suburban sitting in your driveway." He jerked his head in that direction. "And they described the driver as young and blond, wearing a red coat or sweater." He looked pointedly at Vanessa's red sweater. "The incident happened at two forty-five at 618 Juniper Road. The wagon the child was sitting in was bumped, but he's fine, thanks to being wrapped in a coat and blankets. Otherwise we would be taking Vanessa into custody."

"We'll be investigating," Officer Quimby said. "The mother hasn't filed formal charges yet. But after our investigation is complete, your daughter may be charged with negligent operation of a motor vehicle. If the car had been six inches farther up on the sidewalk, it could have been vehicular manslaughter."

"Mom, I didn't do it!" Vanessa said.

Sofia looked at Officer Quimby. "What does this all mean? If she's charged, I mean."

Officer Quimby looked uncomfortable, but he answered formally. "Negligent operation of a motor vehicle is punishable by a fine of $1,000 and imprisonment in the county jail for up to one year, if convicted as an adult."

Sofia gasped. Looking stunned, Vanessa seemed to shrink in upon herself. Sofia moved instinctively to wrap her arms around her daughter, aching with the knowledge that she couldn't make this go away.

2

Chawton Village, England,
July 1812

*J*ane Austen straightened her aching back, replaced her quill pen in the inkstand, and gazed out the window at the drizzly, foggy morning. A closed carriage and an open farm wagon splashed muddy water as they rumbled by the busy crossroads where their cottage was situated. The gray July morning was a direct contrast to the joyful ending she'd just penned. She closed her eyes, ready for a quiet respite . . . but then the door in the hallway banged open.

She had barely covered her manuscript when Mrs. Austen swept into the dining parlor, returning from her visit to the cemetery with their closest neighbor, Mrs. Hatton. Jane's mother was a stout woman, her gray hair surrounding a discontented face. Murmurings and mutterings preceded her as she stomped across the uneven floorboards.

Tugging at her bonnet strings, Mrs. Austen leaned into the fireplace. "Jane, why are you using so little coal? It's no warmer in here than outdoors in the damp." She flung aside her bonnet, and beads of moisture sprayed the floor.

"I barely noticed the cold," Jane said, flexing ink-stained fingers. "Lizzie Bennet and Mr. Darcy came to an understanding this morning—"

"Yes yes." Using the key hanging around her neck, Mrs.

Austen unlocked the tea cupboard, stared at its empty interior, and shut it again. "When will these shortages end? No wood, no coal, no tea."

"At least we don't smoke cigars," Jane said, "so that particular shortage can't hurt us."

"It is not a frivolous matter," Mrs. Austen snapped. "Mrs. Hatton has plenty of coal, she says. Her neighbors make sure she is taken care of, she says. Why does no one take care of us?"

"Mamma, you don't mean that. Just last week, Mr. Dowall gave you a bottle of brandy." While the Austen women weren't drinkers, brandy helped a fever or chills when no medicine was to be had. "Mrs. Hatton lost her husband two years ago and her only son last year. No amount of coal can make up for that."

Mrs. Austen paused in her complaint, and a guilty look passed briefly over her countenance.

England was nine years into the Napoleonic Wars with France, and the United States had also declared war on England. Many families in Chawton Village had sons and husbands who were killed in the wars. Jane had lost count of the memorial services they'd attended at St. Nicholas Church. The Austen family was blessed, though. Two of Jane's five brothers, Charles and Frank, had entered the Naval Academy at fourteen and had been in the thick of the war for years, yet neither had been wounded . . . or worse.

As yet.

Jane's older sister, Cassandra, pushed open the dining parlor door. Nearly forty, Cassandra was aging in a round and pleasant way, as Jane would have expected. She carried a tray of tea and sweet biscuits to the table. "I coaxed one more pot of tea out of the leaves. Weak, perhaps, but still good after a damp walk, Mamma."

Jane made light of it, but sometimes the shortages were hard to bear. Year after year, they couldn't get enough tea, sugar, or medicines, let alone things like silk or lace. Firewood was scarce because so many trees had been cut to build ships, and coal was too costly to buy. Add to that, the British had lost their European markets for the clothing and textiles they produced. A British citizen could stand on England's southern shore and see the coast of France across the channel, but they could no longer trade with them.

Mrs. Austen took her cup of tea and settled into a straight-backed chair. "If only the war would end. How I long to buy enough coal to get the dampness out of the house."

Jane waved her teacup in the air and winked at Cassandra. "Well, Mamma, I have some news that should bring you joy."

"I very much doubt that, Jane. What could you possibly know that I don't know?" Mrs. Austen asked. "You never learn anything useful, hiding away day and night writing your stories."

Jane could not argue with that. For the past year, she'd been at her little table, rewriting and hand-copying a new version of her manuscript retitled *Pride and Prejudice*. She had taken part in very little of the village life, it was true. But to good purpose.

"I may not know what's going on outside these walls at the moment," Jane agreed, "but the fortunes of the Austen women will change very soon."

Cassandra's face was immediately wreathed in a smile. "Jane, have you had news?"

"No, not yet," Jane admitted, "but I'm nearly finished with *Pride and Prejudice*. I know I've buried myself in the cottage for months, but it will pay off soon. I received a miserable ten pounds for *Susan*," she admitted, "but brother Henry thinks, based on what I've made on *Sense and Sensibility*, I can safely predict a new sale of three hundred pounds."

Mrs. Austen squealed and jerked back, spilling tea onto her saucer. "Three hundred pounds. Oh, Jane. Oh, my dear. Think of what we could buy with that." She set her teacup on the dining table. "Tea and sugar. A barrel of flour. Coal enough to banish the chill. New shoes. Maybe even some cloth, if there is any to be had in the shop." She stood and danced over to Jane, enveloping her and nearly squeezing the breath out of her.

Jane grinned at Cassandra over Mamma's shoulder. There was one thing about their mother: Her moods could go from stormy to sunny in seconds. Jane's father, the Reverend George Austen, had died seven years ago while the family had lived at Bath, which accounted for at least some of Mamma's more difficult tendencies in recent years.

Cassandra pulled her shawl tighter around her. "Do you believe you can get so much, Jane?"

Jane shrugged. Her brother—also her literary agent—believed it. "I'd be content with half such a sum," Jane said. "I'll take the manuscript to London soon. I won't trust it to the post." She didn't want to boast, but she felt deep down that *Pride and Prejudice* was the best thing she'd written. The money should go a long way toward making all six of their lives more comfortable.

In addition to her mother and sister, their good friend, Martha Lloyd, also lived with them, although she was away helping an ailing relative that month. And they fed Eliza, their young "maid of all work," plus Thomas, their manservant. They were fortunate to live rent free, thanks to Jane's older brother Edward, who owned the cottage. Jane's mother kept a bountiful vegetable garden, but it still took money for food, fuel, and wages for their two servants. Jane didn't want to reveal how little money was left from the sales of her books. Even if the war hadn't caused shortages, the Austen women would have had to do without many comforts.

Jane rubbed a small circle of moisture off the window. "The drizzle seems to have stopped," she said, "so the fog should lift soon. I feel a need to get out."

"I am not stirring from this chair till I am warm," Mamma

declared. "But you go, Jane. Mrs. Hatton said the shop acquired a shipment of tea yesterday. Do get us some." She glanced around. "Cassandra, fetch my sewing basket."

Jane lifted her summer shawl and bonnet from a hook by the front door, grabbed a wicker basket, and counted the last of the money in her drawstring reticule. It should at least buy Mamma some decent tea.

Swinging her empty basket, she headed outside, where she closed her eyes and breathed deeply, relishing the sweet summer scents of lavender and lilies.

Jane picked her way down the muddy lane toward the village shop that was squeezed between a thatched, black-and-white cottage and the smithy. There, patient carthorses waited in the road. She smiled at the pleasant ring of the blacksmith's anvil and headed to the shop, which was still shrouded in fog.

Being distant from village life the past year had felt strange, and she missed the friendly gossip one could count on in the shop and around sewing circles. She couldn't tell anyone that she, a clergyman's daughter, was writing romantic novels. The horror of being found out nearly left her breathless. Yet she knew people would be glad to see her again. There would be plenty of gossip to be had in the shop over tea and flour and soap.

Maybe she'd see her friend, Anne Powell. The young woman was engaged to a man in the navy, stationed in the Mediterranean. They often talked of him and Frank and Charles, sharing and comparing the precious letters they each wrote home.

Outside the shop, which also housed their posting station, was the Post Office coach, easily identified by its livery. The mail coach guard from Southampton proudly wore his gold-braided scarlet coat with blue lapels and a black hat with a gold band. Maybe there would be a letter today from one of her brothers or Martha Lloyd.

Oh, if only I'd written to Mary and the children, Jane thought, thinking of her brother Frank's family living in the southern port of Southampton. It was too late now. The mail coach would be on its way as soon as the Chawton mail was delivered.

She pushed open the shop door and stepped around several barrels and boxes. Wooden shelves and two glass cabinets containing rows of powders lined the walls. Edmund Watters, the shopkeeper, stood behind a long wooden counter. Like most small village shops, this one was a combination of various individual sellers—grocer, baker, stationer, draper, and chemist.

The shop was filled with small groups of villagers who had more time on their hands than money in their pockets. The barred post office window was empty now, but Jane spotted a man with a large leather pouch behind the screened window. He was murmuring privately to Betsy Watters, who served as postmistress when she wasn't behind the counter with her husband. Jane decided to check the mail after shopping.

Smiling and nodding, Jane wended her way through the chattering groups, hoping to see Anne, but she wasn't there. Even so, Jane knew half a dozen of the women.

"Hello, Mrs. Rutledge. You're looking well. Mamma said you'd had your daughter's family on Sunday. Those little ones must be getting . . . how old now?"

Mrs. Rutledge gave her a stiff smile. "Ten and eight." She dipped a half curtsy. "Good to see you." Ducking behind Jane, she left the shop.

Jane blinked and stared, first confused, then hurt. *How odd.* Turning, she spotted Martha Trim, the woman who brought flowers to the church and whose husband, David, tended the churchyard. Jane touched her arm. "The pink striped daylilies last Sunday were lovely," she said. "So fragrant. I know they helped me concentrate on the sermon."

Martha's eyes widened, and Jane was taken aback. Was that fear she saw there? "What's wrong?" she whispered.

But Martha followed Mrs. Rutledge out the door, her shopping basket still empty.

Jane frowned. Why were the villagers behaving so strangely? Could they be that upset with her for missing local functions and church sewing circles?

A deep clearing of the throat came from behind her. "Miss Austen? May I help you?"

She turned and moved to the counter. "Thank you, Mr. Watters. I do need a few things."

As the war had dragged on, shelves holding material and medicine and grocery items were increasingly bare. But at least she could make Mamma happy today.

"I heard there was tea again," Jane said, "and the Austen women are eager for it. We drank our last weak cup this morning."

"We *had* tea," Mr. Watters said, "but I'm afraid it's gone."

"Already?" Jane's dismay was evident in her voice. She turned around. "Did no one else get tea?" One woman shook her head, but the others stared at the floor, the shelves, or one another—anywhere but at Jane. The only sound was the mail carrier slamming the door on his way out. She turned back to Mr. Watters. "What happened to it?"

He shrugged. "Word gets out when a shipment comes in. It was gone within two hours."

Jane swallowed her disappointment. "I understand. I should have been quicker." She waited, half-expecting someone to step forward and offer to sell her a small amount. But no one did. Instead, they all shuffled toward the door.

Without warning, a heart-wrenching wail filled the small store. "*Noooo-o-o-o!*"

The villagers froze, and Jane's heart pounded faster than the blacksmith's hammer. Over the weeping, she heard Mrs. Watters's soothing voice. "Now now, sit down here. Let me help you."

Who was back there with the shopkeeper's wife?

Then Betsy Watters appeared in the post office window. "Tragedy has come to Chawton Village once more," she announced, her soft voice carrying clearly in the silenced shop. "John March, killed in action."

A collective gasp circled the shop, and tears welled up in Jane's eyes. The Marches were their friends a short walk down the Gosport Road. John, their only son, had gone into the navy a few years after Jane's brother, Frank. They weren't on the same ship, thank heavens.

Jane dreaded taking this news home to her mother. Every time someone was killed in action, Mamma was certain that the next letter would pronounce the death of one of her naval sons. The news of John March's death would put her in bed for days with a sick headache.

The wailing turned to deep, wracking sobs, and Jane felt like she was intruding on her neighbor's private grief. She'd come back later to shop for the other items. The tea had been the only critical thing. With the constant shortages, when would there be more for sale?

Then she felt ashamed. Here she was, questioning how to get along without their tea when Mrs. March faced surviving without her only son. During the months while she'd immersed herself in her writing, Jane could almost pretend England wasn't at war and her two favorite brothers weren't in constant mortal danger.

An involuntary shudder rippled through her. Death close to home ripped away that false comfort.

3

Cabot Falls, Vermont
Present Day

Sofia felt a shudder run through Vanessa's body at the officer's words. "It'll be fine," Sofia whispered. "It's a misunderstanding."

Despite her confident words, Sofia felt dazed, as if she'd been in an accident herself. *Lord, what now? What should we do?* "Have you looked at the car?" she asked the officers. "Wouldn't flattening a trike show scratch marks?"

Officer Wood reached for the door. "Grab your coats, ladies, and we'll examine it together. Officer Quimby will take some photos."

Ryan Quimby shuffled his feet awkwardly, but Sofia was grateful that he was one of the responding officers. He might not be a friend exactly, but at least she remembered him as kind.

Outside, the wind whipped Sofia's scarf as the four of them circled the Suburban. She glanced up once and spotted Pat Cooper scrutinizing the scene from her front window. *Please, not now,* she begged silently. She didn't need her snoopy neighbor, who fancied herself a private eye, to come interrogate and "help" the police do their job.

"If someone ran over a trike, wouldn't the car show it?" Sofia asked again.

"Possibly." Officer Quimby bent down near the front passenger side. He snapped several photos.

Officer Wood hesitated a moment, then dropped down onto

the wet driveway and got on his back. "Hand me the camera," he said, peering under the car. He took several pictures.

Sofia frowned. "What are you doing?"

"Documenting some scratch marks here. They look fairly new."

Sofia squatted beside the car. "What color was the trike?"

"Mostly blue. Some white."

"Do you see any paint like that?"

"No," he admitted, "but hitting it might only scratch the underside."

"Those scratches could be from anything I hit," Sofia said. "After the ice storm a couple of weeks ago, I ran over a limb in the library parking lot. I heard it scrape." Sofia gave Vanessa an encouraging smile.

Officer Wood made no comment as he stood and brushed off his hands and uniform. He squatted next to the front tire on the passenger side. "We need a photo here," he said. "The tire scraped something."

A curb? Sofia felt a sinking in her stomach. "I could have done that," she said. "I have trouble getting close enough to park without hitting the curb."

"Let's go back inside," Officer Wood said.

Sofia led them into the living room, but Officer Quimby asked to sit at the kitchen table. "Makes it easier to fill out forms," he explained. They surprised Wynter, who was getting an apple, but she grabbed it and hurried out.

For several minutes, Officer Quimby asked Vanessa basic questions about her age, grade, classes at school, why she had the family car on Monday, and when she arrived home.

"Can I say something?" Sofia interrupted. "Vanessa's a careful driver, and she's never been in any trouble. She's an excellent student, she's in many extracurriculars, and her teachers like her." She cleared her throat. "She isn't the type to leave the scene of an accident, and certainly not one involving a child."

Officer Wood folded his arms across his chest. "Can you explain how someone reported your license plate number and a description of the driver that fits your daughter?"

"Who is this witness?" Sofia asked. "An anonymous prank?"

Officer Quimby looked almost apologetic. "No. The child's mother and a neighbor witnessed it."

"What was the address again?" Vanessa asked, her voice sounding small and hollow.

"It's 618 Juniper Road," Officer Quimby said.

"I wasn't on that street. I don't even know where that is." Vanessa took a deep breath. "I was at school all day. And after school, I had a committee meeting. I'm on the prom decoration committee. We're doing a luau theme. You know, fake flower leis and rented palm trees."

Sofia watched Vanessa closely, aching for the fear on her daughter's face. But she saw something else there too, something that stirred even more fear in her own heart. Vanessa was protesting too much, as if she had something to hide.

Sofia pushed that thought aside quickly. "Officer Wood, there's obviously been some mistake. My car was at school. Records will show Vanessa was in class."

Officer Wood barely nodded. "And the names of a couple of friends on this committee?" he asked.

"Why?" Vanessa asked.

"So we can verify your whereabouts."

To check your alibi, Sofia mentally translated. It chilled her to think that one of her children even needed an alibi.

"You'll go to their houses too?" Vanessa asked.

Officer Wood barely nodded.

"They'd hate that," she said. "I need to ask them first if I can give their names to you."

"That's not how it's done." Officer Wood crossed his arms across his chest. "It gives suspects time to cook up a story they can agree on."

Sofia snapped her head around and glared at him. *How dare he say such a thing?*

A cascade of emotions flooded Vanessa's face. First she looked scared, then mad, then determined as she clamped her lips together. The officers waited a full minute, but it was clear that she was finished talking.

"Vanessa?" Sofia whispered.

"No, Mom. I didn't cause some accident, and I'm not having the police interrogate my friends." She snapped her fingers. "I know. The faculty advisor for the prom committee will tell you I was at the meeting. It's Mrs. Blythe, the home ec teacher."

Officer Quimby made a note. Then, at some invisible signal, the officers stood, put on their hats, and moved to the door. They stepped out onto the front porch, but Officer Wood turned back around, looking grim. "If the mother files formal charges—and we expect she will—we'll be in touch."

Sofia felt a chill go straight through her, and she knew it wasn't only New England's March wind.

Chawton Village, England
July 1812

Jane tried to shake off her neighbors' chilly reception as she emerged from the shop. The news about John March being killed in action shrank her self-pitying feelings to their proper proportion. Still, if she were honest with herself, she was hurt and puzzled by the villagers' reluctance to include her in their conversation. The shoppers huddled in groups of two or three in the lane, bonnets close together, but no one called out to Jane.

Deep in thought, Jane barely noticed that the fog had burned off, leaving an azure sky overhead. She picked her way around the mud in the lane and headed back to Chawton Cottage. Feeling bedraggled, she was sure her petticoat was six inches deep in mud.

"Jane! Jane Austen!"

Jane glanced up, surprised to already be opposite the Powell cottage. Young Anne was leaning out the open window, her face in shadow from the overhanging thatched roof. Jane always found her amiable and full of good sense. It revived her spirits. Even if others were cool to her, Anne would always be her warm, bubbly self.

Jane waited for a donkey cart to pass, then zigzagged around potholes and puddles to cross the street. Anne disappeared from the window and threw open the front door. "Come in, come in." She stepped back into the dim hall. "I haven't seen you out and about for ages."

"I know," Jane said, untying her bonnet strings. "I have become quite the hermit this year, but I am determined to change that. Being outside this morning feels good."

"Your countenance says otherwise." Anne leaned her head to one side, making her blond curls dance. "Were you at the post office?" She gripped Jane's arm. "Have you had bad news about Charles or Frank?" Her voice rose in alarm and empathy for the worry that was always beneath the surface for military families.

"No, no, Frank and Charles are well, from what we know." Jane set her empty basket down by the door and then followed Anne into their warm sitting room. "But it was bad news for the March family this morning."

"Not John?"

"I fear so. Killed in action."

"Oh no!" Anne wrung her delicate hands together. "Where was he fighting?"

Jane knew what Anne feared. Had John March died fighting in the Mediterranean where her fiancé, George Crawford, was helping guard the port at Genoa?

"John died in a fight with the Americans, not Napoleon. But I don't know where."

Anne collapsed in a nearby chair, her relief almost palpable. "I don't know what I would do if—"

"Don't dwell on that," Jane said, drawing on many years of experience with brothers in the navy. "'Sufficient unto the day is the evil thereof.'"

Anne forced a smile. "You're right, of course." And then she broke into a genuine smile of delight. "I almost forgot why I called to you. I have something for you to see."

Grateful for a turn in the conversation, Jane made herself comfortable in a rocker, adjusting the embroidered pillow in the small of her back. Her extensive hours hunched over her writing desk lately had left her with an old crone's spine in the body of someone only thirty-seven.

Anne was gone barely a moment. When she returned with her arms full of material, her mother followed. Mrs. Powell, a plump, jolly woman who hardly seemed like she could be the mother of her tiny slip of a daughter, had a personality that quickly reverted to optimism no matter what her circumstances. Jane so appreciated that frame of mind. Her own frequently complaining Mamma could take lessons in daily comportment from Mrs. Powell.

"Is this *satin*?" Jane asked, astonished. She hadn't seen white satin such as that since before the war.

"You're right to be shocked," Mrs. Powell said, dancing around her daughter. For such a large woman, she was remarkably light on her feet. And what feet they were. Jane would have sworn she spotted new leather boots as her long skirts swished by. "Young

George also sent our Anne this." Her plump fingers held yards of the most exquisite French lace.

Jane *was* shocked. How had that been possible?

Giggling, Anne laid the heavy satin in Jane's lap. "It's to be for my wedding dress when the war is over." Despite her worn day dress and the obviously repaired apron, Anne's eyes glowed. Jane imagined she was picturing herself sweeping down the church aisle, trailing a long satin train.

Jane touched the material carefully and then handed it back. She didn't want to snag it on her rough skin or stain it with the ever-present ink on her fingers.

"Tell me all about it," she said.

Jane's gaze traveled back and forth between mother and daughter as they stumbled over each other's words to tell what had happened three days before.

"My darling George's ship put into Portsmouth for a few hours—"

"To pick up more recruits from the Naval Academy—"

"But he was only in port a few hours—"

"So he found a traveler to bring the package to our Anne, and not only that—"

"He also sent things for Mamma and Papa—"

"Brandy. Can you believe it? We want to give Mrs. Austen a bottle to tuck away for the winter chills."

"I hardly know what to say," Jane said. That was true for more than one reason. Of course she was happy for Anne. How wonderful to have something surprisingly good happen in such tough times. But something didn't smell right. If it were possible for navy men to do this, why hadn't Frank or Charles sent the Austens any such packages? Not satin and lace, of course, but dress material or shoes or tea? She hadn't heard of Frank sending his wife, Mary, and their three children any such packages either.

Still, what an overwhelming gift. Certainly more than any of them had seen in years, even for Christmas.

"I can't wait to get started," Anne said. "I've almost decided on a pattern."

"Do not make haste," Jane warned. "A gift like this comes along once in a lifetime."

Mrs. Powell bounced on the balls of her feet. "I'm afraid to cut into it myself. One wrong snip . . ." She made cutting motions with her plump fingers. "We must be very careful."

"Will you help?" Anne asked, eyes aglow.

"Help? You mean, to make the wedding dress?"

"Of course. The sewing will take many hours, but we can talk." She gripped Jane's arm. "With Charles and Frank in the navy too, you understand when I talk about George." A cloud passed over her face. "Talking helps keep my spirits up."

Jane's heart sank. She wished Anne hadn't asked her. Jane was ready to prepare *Pride and Prejudice* to submit to her publisher in London. It would require many more hours to create a clean copy of the manuscript. Her hands would be much too cramped from the writing to then sew. She wished she could tell Anne why she had to refuse, but her brothers had emphasized repeatedly that she must not reveal her identity and shame the family.

"I'm sorry, but I won't have the time that would require," she said.

Anne gently withdrew her hand and stepped back. "I thought you were happy for me."

"You know I am," Jane said, "even though I am destined to be an old maid." It was her choice, but unless she could marry for love—like Anne—she much preferred spinsterhood and arranging marriages for her heroines. Noting Anne's crestfallen expression, Jane hurried on. "Could I instead sew something personal for you to carry on your wedding day? With a square of the silk and lace to trim it, I could create a special handkerchief for you."

Mrs. Powell nodded. "Could you do your whitework embroidery on it?"

"I think so," Jane said. "I've done it on muslin and cambric. If I take my time, I could do a design on the silk."

Jane loved doing white-on-white needlework, using white thread on white material to create a pattern. She used various techniques to make the patterns stand out and give her whitework pieces a sculptural quality.

Anne chewed her lower lip. "I guess I'll have to agree," she said, "but only if you add your initials."

Jane thought a moment. "In one corner, I won't do a whitework design. Instead, I'll sew 'In friendship, J.A.' there."

Anne smiled then. "I'd like that. But anytime that you're not too busy, I hope you'll come and sew with us. You're always welcome."

Jane gave Anne a brief hug, took the square of silk and piece of lace that was cut for her, and left.

Although the fog had fully lifted, Jane's spirits sank. She hated to disappoint Anne, but she couldn't sacrifice the hours it would take to help sew a wedding dress. Might she have to go against her family's wishes and reveal to her neighbors that she—a clergyman's spinster daughter—was writing stories of romance for publication?

Jane grimaced, her expression protected by her bonnet. If she was receiving the cold shoulder now, she could only imagine the freezing temperatures if her fellow villagers knew her secret.

4

Cabot Falls, Vermont
Present Day

Keeping the secret was hard, but Sofia waited until the children were in bed to break the news to Jim. For a solid minute he sat motionless at the kitchen table, hands wrapped around his coffee mug.

"Say something," Sofia said.

"I can't believe this." He pushed his coffee away. "What if we get sued?"

Sofia gasped. "Sued? Why?"

"People do it all the time, especially if there was a child involved."

"But nobody got hurt."

"That won't matter. They can sue for 'emotional distress.' Unscrupulous lawyers take cases like that on a contingency fee." He rubbed a hand across his six o'clock shadow. "Innocent or not, it would cost a lot to defend Vanessa in court."

Sofia reached across the table and squeezed his hand. "Vanessa swears she was at school during the time of the accident, and I believe her. There must be some mistake."

Jim stared off into space for a moment. "It could still have been your car that jumped the curb." His teeth clenched, making his jaw square. "She could have loaned the car to someone. Like Ethan maybe."

"Do you think so?" Sofia asked. Ethan Hall, Vanessa's

boyfriend, was hardly likely to fit the description given to the police. But they had to consider every possibility.

"One way to find out. I'll check his attendance record tomorrow and see if he made it to track practice after school." Jim pushed back his chair. "If Vanessa gave him your keys, she's grounded. And if the police don't take her license, I will."

Sofia slept little that night. The next morning, after dropping the kids off at school, she swung onto the highway instead of going home. Her dad, a widower since Sofia was four, lived only an hour away, and she needed to talk to him about Vanessa.

She drove through a rural area and past a dairy farm, an apple orchard, a blueberry field, and acres of leafless sugar maple trees. They'd be tapped to make maple syrup before long.

Twenty minutes later, she heard her phone chime. She pulled over, eager to read the text message. It was from Jim. "Ethan at school all day. Went to track too. Talk later."

Well, that's good, she thought, but they still knew nothing. As she drove, Sofia's mind repeated the officers' words and each of Vanessa's answers in a never-ending loop.

At the next road sign, she took the turn toward the small Vermont town where her sixty-five-year-old father had retired. After Sofia's mother died, Lou Nelson had immersed himself in his work as a physicist. He'd never needed anyone besides Sofia, her two older sisters, and, eventually, all the grandchildren they'd given him. Until recently.

Now he occasionally went to lunch or the movies with lady friends—"emphasis on *friends*," he always said. Even so, it felt odd to Sofia after all these years of having her dad to herself. When he'd brought his latest friend, Lois Randall, to Gina's house for a big birthday celebration, Gina had been speechless. They'd all been subdued, and for a loud, sometimes argumentative Italian family, the quiet was awkward. Lois hadn't seemed to notice, but she wasn't familiar with their typical dynamic. She'd talked at length with Gina's husband, the state senator, and Rosa's husband, the heart surgeon.

Sofia was glad Lois still worked for PBS's history department. Sofia wanted some time alone with her dad. Too old and too big to sit on Dad's knee, she still needed a hug from the wiry man whose sharp blue eyes always saw through her "I'm fine, Dad" when she wasn't.

When she pulled in, she was surprised to see the double garage door open. Her father was lifting down cardboard boxes for his annual spring cleaning, after which he would put them all back instead of throwing anything away.

Sofia got out and hurried into the garage. "Hi, Dad." She hugged him, letting her eyes adjust after being out in the bright sun.

"To what do I owe this great pleasure?" He leaned back to study her. "Is everything all right?"

Before she could answer, the door connecting the garage to the kitchen swung open. Dressed in a baby-blue tracksuit, Lois stepped down into the garage. "I found those new garbage bags." She smiled in surprise. "Hello. Sofia, isn't it?"

Sofia forced her lips into a stiff smile. *What is Lois doing here so early?*

Her dad must have read the question in her eyes. "Lois came over this morning to help me clean this out, once and for all. I can barely find room for the car, lawn mower, and snow blower these days."

"Got to take advantage of these sunny days," Lois agreed. She picked up a box of odds and ends. "I'll stick these in my car, if you're sure you won't need them." She carried the box on her hip to a gray car parked across the street and was back in thirty seconds.

"Everything okay?" Dad asked again, brushing back his thinning blond hair.

"Oh sure." Sofia glanced over the boxes of childhood board games, folded lawn chairs that were coming apart, and a flat volleyball. She wasn't going to talk about the police questioning Vanessa, not in front of his lady friend. "I hadn't seen you for a while, so I thought I'd treat myself to a visit when you and I could get a word in edgewise."

Her dad laughed at that. At the boisterous holiday get-togethers, the two of them usually gave up and let the others talk.

"Do you want some coffee? We don't have to do this now."

"I don't want to interrupt," Sofia said, feeling like a third wheel. "We can chat while I help sort."

"No you're not." Her dad unfolded a redwood lawn chair that was still in good shape. "Sit."

While he sorted through bent nails and rusty screws he'd dumped out of old baby food jars, Sofia told him about starting the research on the third quilt square. "I know it sounds impossible, but that signature is in English, and Jane Austen was known to do embroidery work."

Dad bounced a handful of long screws in his palm. "Since the quilt is from Nonna's Italian side, that doesn't sound too likely." Then he gave her a wink. "Maybe you're related to Jane Austen on my side of the family."

"How do you figure that?"

"Nelson is a good British name, and—"

"Surely you know the history of your own name." Lois turned from where she was sorting through dusty file boxes of papers. "We did a series on Napoleon at PBS. Your maiden name—Nelson—goes back to the British admiral Lord Horatio Nelson. He's best remembered for the Battle of Trafalgar, in which he pushed back Napoleon's fleet but was himself killed. What a time for the British navy—the war with Napoleon, the War of 1812 with America, pirates galore, and all that smuggling!" She pressed two fingers against her forehead. "Nelson died before that, of course, in 1805, I believe. There's a big statue of him in Trafalgar Square, in the center of London."

Sofia assumed she was trying to be helpful, but she came across as a show-off. "I think Jane Austen's books were written after 1805 though," Sofia said.

"Yes, but they learned embroidery as children, didn't they? When was she born?"

Sofia thought for a moment. "Late 1775, I think."

"Well, there you have it then."

Her dad grinned at Sofia. *I stand corrected*, Sofia thought, wondering exactly what she was to have learned from that little lecture.

Half an hour later, Sofia felt she'd stayed long enough to be friendly, and she made her departure. Waving as she backed out of the driveway, Sofia headed south. As she drove, her artist's heart longed to stop and paint the scenes before her: the dark winter hardwoods, the evergreens on the hills, the red barns, and the weathered woodsheds.

But soon she reached the Cabot Falls exit and turned the car toward home and the trouble still waiting.

Chawton Village, England
July 1812

As Jane hurried toward home to her family still waiting for their tea, she was no longer eager to meet anyone in the lane. Pairs of women gossiped in their gardens over back fences, but no one glanced Jane's way. It felt deliberate, but perhaps her experience in the shop was coloring her perception.

She'd left the cottage only an hour ago, expecting some friendly gossip at the shop while making her purchases, and then a chance to catch up on village news with Anne. Instead, she'd been shunned. At least it felt that way. Then she'd disappointed her young friend, despite the offer to make her a special embroidered handkerchief.

Most of all, the weight of hearing about John March settled on her heavily, reminding Jane of her own brothers who risked their lives every day to protect England from attack.

When she arrived at Chawton Cottage, she couldn't force herself to go in. Not immediately. She wasn't up to one of Mamma's theatrical dramas about John March and the lack of tea. Jane needed to soothe her own wounded heart first. She scanned the dining parlor windows, the sitting room window, and the bedchamber windows in the upper story of the house. Could she be that lucky? She didn't see a family member or the maid or manservant anywhere, so she picked up her speed.

She would walk to the end of the village near the great house and stop at St. Nicholas's. Behind the church, amongst the oldest graves, she often sat under the shade of an ancient yew to think about her stories without interruption. Today, though, she felt the need for a holy place to pray for her brothers' safety.

Across the road, at Chawton Pond, three small boys in ragged, muddy trousers held a rock-skipping contest. They ignored her as her skirts brushed against the tall weeds that bloomed in the ditch. Jane's agitated heart felt as if it could burst. Instead of walking sedately along the lane like the spinster she was, how she longed to leave her worries behind and run through a field purple with bluebells and let the heady scent envelop her.

But no, the best she could manage today was a pensive stroll to the church to pray and settle her heart before going home.

Jane didn't go inside the church but followed the walk around toward the back. A new grave would be added at the side of the church for John March if they had a body to ship home. Then Mrs. March, like so many other village women, would plant an

English rosebush and water it often with her tears.

Jane continued on around the building and out of sight of the road. She walked past grave monuments and stone crosses too worn down by time and weather to be readable. Some still stood upright, but many tilted, and others had fallen over. At the far back, several stones at odd angles were surrounded by uncut grass and brambles. It was no surprise really. St. Nicholas had been around since the 1200s, so those buried in the oldest section had no one left to tend their graves. And old David Trim, the church's caretaker, could barely keep up.

Jane felt the sticky July heat now, and the cold stone bench under the tree was welcome. She breathed deeply and closed her eyes, grateful for the quiet there that, if she waited long enough, always brought her peace.

She had nearly dozed off when she was startled by voices. Voices that were quite nearby, she realized. Jane sat erect and straightened her skirt, but no one came around to the back of the church. Although their words carried clearly, she couldn't make out the identities of the women who were speaking.

"Poor Mrs. March. Poor, poor thing," one crooned. "At least John died a hero."

"Maybe, maybe not," another woman said. "My Henry heard that he wasn't killed in battle at all."

The first woman gasped. "That can't be true. I was in the shop when the letter came."

"But did anyone actually *read* the letter?"

There was a short silence. "No, but we wouldn't ask, would we?"

"My Henry said he was captured by an American ship and he gave up."

"No."

"He defected and agreed to fight on the American side so he wouldn't be taken prisoner."

Jane found that she was holding her breath, and her chest hurt. She knew from Frank that defecting was a common occurrence since America had declared war on England and added to the navy's burdens. But if John March had actually defected and he was caught, he'd be hanged.

The second woman finally said, "Perhaps the Marches would rather mourn John as a dead hero than admit he's a traitor."

The first woman's voice faded, and Jane strained to catch her words as she heard them walking away. "Well, if it's true—and I'm not saying I believe it—John March is only *one* kind of traitor in Chawton."

Jane sat stiffly on the stone bench, shivering in the July heat, long after their shuffling footsteps died away. The peace she had sought was annihilated by the woman's last shocking statement. What did she mean, "only *one* kind of traitor"?

What was going on beneath the surface of their quiet little village? And why did she get the distinct impression that it was being kept from her?

"But I want my other lace fichu!" Mamma cried. "This has a hole in it, and I won't wear it to church."

Jane rolled her eyes at Cassandra. If they didn't leave now, they'd be late to St. Nicholas's again. Last week Mamma had had so many vapors and faux fainting spells that they hadn't made it to church at all.

"Here, Mamma," Cassandra said, adjusting the fichu around her neck. "Stand still. I'll fix my brooch over the snagged place, and it won't show. Nobody will know it's there."

"*I'll* know it's there, and I'm not nobody," Mamma retorted. "I'm so weary of this war. Will it never end so a body can be decently clothed again?"

Jane tapped her foot impatiently as she waited by the open door, clutching her Testament. The welcome summer sun warmed her upturned face. It had been a damp summer, and the day was cool for July.

At last Mamma was satisfied with her appearance, and the three women set off down the lane. It was only a ten-minute walk to the church, but Jane increased her speed. Already the bell was ringing and the lane was empty. She gritted her teeth, trying to regain her Sunday peace, but she hated walking in when the service had already begun.

Jane leaned close to Cassandra. "I think she does this by design in order to make an entrance."

"Shhh." Cassandra glanced at Mamma. "I'm sure you're wrong."

Jane bit her tongue. Cassandra was the dearest, sweetest sister, but she could be so naïve.

Ten minutes later they stepped from the warming sun into the cool church. Wooden pews ran down either side of the half-full nave, and several worshippers turned at the sound of the heavy wooden door closing. Jane avoided the vicar's frown as he made announcements from the pulpit. After Jane's eyes adjusted to the dim interior of the church, she spotted a row of wicker picnic baskets filled with food in the vestibule.

"Is there a picnic on the lawn after church?" she whispered.

Cassandra shrugged. "Maybe it was announced last week when we weren't here."

And no one mentioned it to us either, Jane thought. Well, this would be a fortunate time to reestablish her friendships in the village. "You two go in," she said, her voice covered by the organ's introduction to a hymn. "I'll hurry home and have Eliza put together a basket of food to share. Can I bring the Bakewell tart?"

Mamma frowned. "Perhaps a quarter of it."

Cassandra countered her suggestion. "Bring at least half. If you bring the whole thing, I'll make Mamma another one tonight."

Jane retied her bonnet and headed back outdoors and down the lane. She could return with a picnic basket before the sermon was much under way.

Relishing being alone on the road, Jane untied her bonnet and let it hang down her back by its strings. Glancing ahead and behind to be sure she was unobserved, she picked up her skirts and ran, arriving at the Chawton Cottage crossroads in half the time it would have taken her otherwise. The lane was deserted except for a farm wagon parked down the street, its tired horse hanging its head. Everyone was in church—or home in bed, in the case of the non-churchgoing men.

Jane had just reached their cottage when a movement down the Gosport Road caught her eye. A huge, rough-looking character with a full black beard emerged from the Rutledges' cottage. Jane slipped out of sight around the corner of Chawton Cottage and then peered through the climbing roses.

Who in the world was that coming out of her neighbors' front door?

5

Cabot Falls, Vermont
Present Day

"Come in, come in." Two hours after returning from seeing her dad, Sofia stood in her open front door. The midafternoon sunshine was warm despite the brisk temperatures.

Carrying easels and paints, her best friends, Julie Butler and Marla Dixon, trooped into the foyer. Calling themselves the Pinot Painters, they'd all been painting together for six years, ever since meeting at a local art show.

"Here you go," Julie said, handing Sofia their traditional bottle of wine.

"Go ahead and set up." Sofia waved the bottle in the direction of the four-season room. "Today I'm footloose and fancy-free. I don't need to pick up anyone. Jim's taking the kids with him when he gets the oil changed in his car. He said he'd oversee homework while they waited."

"What a guy." Marla pulled off her hat and set her wavy blond hair free. A young widow with a generous heart and beautiful smile, she'd been Sofia's dear friend for years. As head librarian at the Cabot Falls Public Library, she'd also been great at helping her research the origins of Nonna's quilt.

Next to Marla, Julie looked like a model, with her tall, curvy figure, stunning red hair, and green eyes. Her looks coupled with her chatty personality and infectious laugh made her a good fit for her marketing job at a public relations firm.

Sofia loved her weekly get-togethers with Marla and Julie. Today she especially looked forward to forgetting her problems for a couple of hours. She had decided not to tell them about Vanessa's situation yet. She hoped the mistake would be righted soon.

Following her friends to the four-season room, Sofia caught a quick conspiratorial look pass between them. "What's up?"

Julie did a quick two-step around the room before answering. "Let's have dessert first today. I'm about to burst with the news."

"Tell me," Sofia said. But neither friend would divulge the secret until they were settled in the living room, Bakewell tart in hand. "Okay, what's up? You both look like cats in the cream."

Marla waved her fork at Julie. "You tell her before you bust."

"It's what we've been waiting for." Julie leaned forward eagerly. "One of the tourist shops on the town square is empty now. We could rent it and sell our art there."

Sofia smiled uncertainly. Cabot Falls was a place where boutique shops filled with local artisan products lined the streets of the quaint downtown square. Julie knew how to publicize, but a shop? "I'm probably more interested in developing my catering business," Sofia said. "The art we do together is for fun. I doubt that mine would sell."

"But a shop on the square would be perfect for so many things. It wouldn't have to be only our art. You could bring in your fancy desserts to sell too." Julie crossed her legs and swung one foot like a metronome. "The owner of Twin Oaks Antiques on the corner of Main and Pine had a severe stroke yesterday. I'm sorry for him, really. But he'll probably have to break his lease, according to the chamber-of-commerce grapevine."

Marla paused with a forkful of dessert halfway to her lips. "They won't have any trouble finding someone else to take over the lease."

Julie's head bobbed in agreement. "That's why we need to move fast."

Sofia hesitated. Julie always had her finger on the pulse of the Cabot Falls Chamber of Commerce. It was part of her job. But take over a lease? That sounded like it would take a lot of money up front.

"What do you think, Marla?" Sofia asked. Despite having a job and a teenager, Marla had more empty hours to fill than either she or Julie did.

"I won't deny that it sounds exciting," Marla said, choosing her words carefully. "I'd love something new and creative, a new dream." She laughed then. "I'd love to sell the art projects crowding my house to some tourists too."

Sofia could understand that. "It's exciting to think about," she agreed.

"But we can't think too long," Julie said. "In fact—"

"I'm home," Vanessa called, then slammed the front door.

Sofia heard various things drop—backpack in the hall, shoes kicked off by the door—before Vanessa appeared in the living room doorway.

"Hey Vanessa," Julie called. "You're looking stunning, as always."

Vanessa gave an embarrassed laugh and let her shoulder-length blond hair fall over her face, half-hiding her green eyes. Petite and thin, she looked undernourished—*like all her friends*, Sofia thought, but she had learned to keep her opinion to herself. Vanessa shot a questioning glance at Sofia that clearly asked, *Do they know?* Sofia gave a nearly imperceptible shake of the head and saw Vanessa relax.

"I'm surprised you're home already." Sofia glanced at their grandfather clock. "Didn't Dad pick you up?"

"I didn't want to go to that gross oil place," Vanessa said, "so he dropped me off. I promised to go straight upstairs and not bother you." She snatched a piece of Bakewell tart off Sofia's plate. "Oh, hey, today two kids in lit class offered to buy your *Pride and Prejudice* drawings. Could you sketch a few more? Even the teacher wants one."

"Really?" Flattered and surprised, Sofia nodded. "But I won't charge for them."

"What's all this?" Julie asked. "What drawings?"

"Caricatures." Sofia explained about their *Pride and Prejudice* marathon on Sunday. "Like this." She reached for her sketch pad behind her chair and drew a quick caricature of the arrogant clergyman, Mr. Collins.

Julie clapped when she saw it. "There you go! That's how you can turn your art into a paying job."

Sofia raised an incredulous eyebrow.

"I'm on to something here." Julie's eyes danced with excitement. "Caricatures would draw a crowd into the shop."

"I don't know."

"You could set up your easel on the sidewalk outside our art shop and offer to do caricatures for tourists walking by. Look how fast you did this one. Naturally, the people you sketched would come into the shop after you told them you had Bakewell tarts in there for sale." Julie punctuated this with a big bite of her pie.

Sofia carefully kept her expression neutral. "Well, I'll think about it," she said. But inwardly she recoiled. She absolutely hated the idea. *Talk about commercialization of art!*

Marla suddenly reached out and grabbed Sofia's arm. "I've got another great idea. Your grandmother's quilt."

"What about it?" What did that have to do with opening a shop?

"We could have a special grand opening and display your antique quilt in the store, maybe for one evening, a special showing. You could serve dessert too. Even if you haven't discovered the ancestors of all the squares by then, you could talk about the ones you'd researched."

Sofia was speechless. She knew her older sisters would hit the roof if she attempted such a thing. Imagine—strangers touching the priceless fabrics! Besides, as valuable as it was, Sofia wasn't about to advertise to the general public that she owned it. Nonna had hinted that if its whereabouts became known, certain greedy characters would go to great lengths to get it.

"I've only just begun on the third square," she said, "and I'd need my family's okay before I could do that."

"But it's your quilt, isn't it, Mom?" Vanessa asked.

"Yes, but . . ." Sofia trailed off. Unless she wanted to bring the wrath of her sisters down on her head, Sofia knew the quilt had better remain where it was, wrapped and hidden away from strangers.

Chawton Village, England
July 1812

Jane peered through the climbing roses at the stranger who'd emerged from her neighbor's cottage, a wrapped bundle in his arms. Glancing both ways, he laid it carefully in the back of the wagon, then checked the lane again. Jane pushed aside a cluster of roses for a clearer view. Who was that giant of a man? And what was he doing at the Rutledge cottage? If she hadn't seen the entire Rutledge family in their church pew in the nave, she would have feared that the stranger was abducting one of their small children.

Jane watched, barely breathing.

The man got into his wagon and drove four cottages down the Gosport Road, then stopped again. After scanning both ends of the lane, the stranger marched to the Kearleys' front door. Without knocking, he pushed right in. Jane was fairly sure she'd seen the Kearleys at church too.

Why were the cottages unlocked? Were her neighbors expecting him while they were in church?

The man emerged from the second cottage carrying another wrapped bundle. Then it dawned on her. Whoever he was, the man was *stealing* from poor families he knew were in church.

She burst out of hiding, picked up her skirts, and raced down the middle of the lane. "Stop!" she yelled. "Sir, what are you doing?"

The man turned, shocked at the sight of her, then bolted to the wagon where he tossed the bundle in and then climbed up. Standing, he whipped the horse and took off, wheels clattering until he rounded a corner, out of sight.

Jane forgot about fixing a food basket and raced back to the church. Heart pounding, she burst into the service. She raced down the center aisle, then turned and faced the parishioners. The stunned vicar halted his sermon in midsentence.

Gasping for breath, Jane said, "You must leave! Your cottages are being robbed while you sit here!"

The organist's hands crashed down on the keys, and the discord added to the pandemonium that broke out.

"Listen! Please!" Jane cried over the noise. "Kearleys and Rutledges, I witnessed a man walk into your cottages and carry out your belongings. He drove off in a wagon at high speed."

Both Mr. Rutledge and Mr. Kearley jumped up and started for the door, then glanced at each other and faltered. After a short pause, Mr. Kearley faced the worshippers. "My home was locked up tight, I'm sure, but we'll go check. You all stay here."

Jane straightened her bonnet and dress and then joined Cassandra and Mamma in the Austen family pew. Now that the crisis had passed, she felt a bit ridiculous about how she'd handled it. Had she really needed to disrupt the whole church service? By her glares, Mamma was apparently thinking the same thing. It wasn't the first time Jane had embarrassed her mother. Undoubtedly it wouldn't be the last.

The vicar settled everyone, shook back his graying hair, and raked fingers through his goatee. After a moment, he spoke about laying up treasures where moth and rust could not corrupt and thieves could not find. Jane wondered if that would be any comfort to the two families who'd been robbed.

After the shortened service, both Mr. Rutledge and Mr. Kearley stepped into the nave.

The vicar motioned them to come forward. "I'm sure we're all eager to hear what you found."

Mr. Rutledge spoke. "As far as we can tell, nothing is missing. In fact, both our doors were still locked."

Jane's mouth dropped open, and many parishioners swung around to stare at her. "They're lying," Jane whispered to her sister.

"But why would they?" Cassandra whispered back.

Jane didn't know, but when they picnicked on the church lawn, she intended to find out. *I know what I saw.*

Jane gathered her Testament and the prayer book that had fallen to the floor, then waited until most of the churchgoers had filed out before she stepped into the aisle. As they neared the door, she saw that all the food baskets were gone. She could still run home and get that tart to share.

But first, she must apologize to the vicar.

"Think nothing of it, my dear." He tugged at his black coat, which appeared tight around the neck. "You alerted us to an evil you believed you saw. I am grateful to the Almighty that it turned out to be a false alarm." He patted her hand. "'To err is human; to forgive, divine.'"

Jane bit her tongue hard, aided by the hard pinch Cassandra gave her elbow. While she agreed with the English poet, she had done nothing in error. But arguing with the vicar would do no good. Nor would it help to call two of his parishioners bold-faced liars.

She walked outside with Mamma and Cassandra. "Mamma,"

Jane said, "I never got the tart to share, but I'll get it now. Go ahead and start without me."

"Start what?" Cassandra said, surprise in her voice. "And where?"

Jane watched from the step as children hiked down the drive and turned away from Chawton while other families followed in donkey carts, wagons, and pony traps.

"Where are they going?" Mamma asked.

"I don't know." Jane grabbed the hand of a little girl racing by. "Susan, where is everyone headed?"

"The Way farm to picnic by their stream. I'm using James's fishing pole!"

As she raced on by, Mercy Way came forward. She sounded confident, but she would not look Jane in the eye. "I know you're too busy to join our little picnic," she said, staring in the vicinity of Jane's ear. "With you being under the squire's care, we understand that spending time with the common folk is tedious."

Jane felt as though she had been physically slapped across the face. Her brother Edward, as Squire of Chawton, had certainly made their lives easier with his endowments, but she, her mother and sister had never treated their neighbors as "common folk." She turned with basket in hand and swept across the church lawn to climb into her horse-drawn carriage.

"Oh, Jane, now see what you've done," Mamma said, wiping her eyes with her lawn handkerchief.

Jane was stunned at the public snub, especially since she'd alerted two of the "common" families that they'd been robbed.

Was she being ostracized for turning down invitations in the past year while reworking *Pride and Prejudice* for publication? Writing in secret made it hard to explain when she avoided social events. Did they think she showed an abominable sort of conceited independence? Maybe, but that didn't explain why Cassandra and her mother were being treated poorly as well.

Jane followed them down the drive and turned the opposite way toward home. So much for her plan to reestablish friendships in the village. Jane tried to shake off the depression that threatened to settle over her, but the shine had gone out of the day.

Until she noticed something that gave her a lift. "Cassandra, look."

At the crossroads, two cottages down the Winchester Road, was Willie Lumb. Although twenty, with his gangly, wiry limbs, he could pass for fifteen. He rarely attended church, but there he was, giving a burlap bag to the Widow Hatton. She often depended on generous people to keep body and soul together.

Despite missing several teeth, her smile was bright. She squealed in delight as she pulled various items from the bag. Jane smiled as Widow Hatton unwrapped a towel to find a loaf of bread, and from the bottom of the bag she pulled a large fish. She'd be eating a sumptuous Sunday dinner today.

"How kind he is," Cassandra said.

Mamma sniffed. "Certainly cut from a better piece of cloth than his father. Must get his good heart from his mother's side."

Jane determined to focus on Willie's kindness instead of the cold treatment from the villagers. At least someone was acting like a good Christian on the Sabbath.

Still, something very odd was going on in Chawton Village. It was more than being snubbed by the offended women. She'd distinctly seen Mrs. Rutledge and Mrs. Kearley before they turned their backs on her, and they had looked terrified.

6

Cabot Falls, Vermont
Present Day

After the Pinot Painters packed up their art materials and went home, Sofia headed to the kitchen to fix supper. Nothing relaxed her like cooking.

As chilly as the day was, she'd planned a hearty tomato minestrone soup with croutons. Most of the ingredients Sofia had cut up earlier: the thick-cut prosciutto, zucchini, celery, carrots, and onion. She added four cups of chicken stock, some cannellini beans, and whole-wheat penne pasta. While it all simmered with bay leaves and basil, she made croutons from four thick slices of Italian bread and freshly grated Parmigiano-Reggiano cheese.

She was readying the homemade yeast rolls to slip into the oven later when the doorbell rang. Heart pounding, she went to answer the door.

Officer Wood stood on her doorstep. In the driveway, her neighbor Pat Cooper had cornered Ryan Quimby, Pat's former English pupil. From what Sofia could hear, she still had the power to reduce him to a stutter.

"Yes?" Sofia said. "Have you found who jumped the curb yesterday?"

"We do have new information." Officer Wood's expression gave away nothing. "Can we come in?"

Soon Sofia and both officers were seated in the kitchen. She felt a sick sense of déjà vu.

"Mrs. Parker," Officer Wood said, "we talked to the geography teacher at school today who has Vanessa for class after lunch. He said that she left class sick and reported to the nurse's office yesterday."

Sofia's stomach twisted. This was certainly news. She waited, removing her clenched hands from the tabletop to her lap, out of sight.

"The school nurse's records show that Vanessa did show up there but reported feeling better within fifteen minutes and said she would go back to class."

Sofia relaxed a fraction but wished Jim would walk in the door that minute.

Officer Wood paused. The silence stretched out like a taut rubber band until Sofia thought she might snap.

"And?" she finally said.

"The teachers of her last two classes never saw her. They didn't report her absent since Vanessa's classmates said she was in the nurse's office."

A noise from the living room made Sofia twist around. "Vanessa? Is that you?"

No answer. Then Vanessa appeared from around the corner. Sofia had to admire her unconcerned stance when the terror was clear in her eyes.

Sofia cleared her throat. "It appears that you skipped classes yesterday. Would you like to explain to these two officers about the discrepancy in your story?"

Vanessa looked at Sofia instead of the officers. "I *was* at the meeting after school. We—I—came back for it. But I wasn't even on the street where that accident happened. I didn't lie about that."

Officer Quimby's voice was kind but insistent. "When you left the nurse's office, where did you go?"

Vanessa had the look of a wild animal caught in a trap. "It doesn't matter where I went. I wasn't responsible for the car going up on the curb."

"We have other avenues to explore." Officer Wood closed his notebook and slipped it into his shirt pocket. "It won't take ten minutes of cross-checking to see who else was missing yesterday."

Pure misery filled Vanessa's eyes, but she remained silent.

"Vanessa, please tell us where you were. And who's your alibi? I admire loyalty, but this time, yours is misplaced."

"Mrs. Parker," Officer Wood interjected, "your daughter doesn't want to admit having a friend in the car with her because it's a direct violation of her junior driver's license. Until she's eighteen, Vermont prohibits her from driving with her friends unless an adult is with her in the front seat." He cleared his throat. "If we prove she was transporting another student, she will lose her license."

Sofia blinked, taking it all in. "Vanessa?" she asked.

"I didn't do it, Mom. Isn't my word enough?"

Sofia studied her older daughter's face, and every instinct was to believe her. She glanced at Officer Wood. She feared his gut instincts were telling him something entirely different.

"Mrs. Parker," Officer Wood said, "today the boy's mother filed a formal complaint. When the paperwork is done, Vanessa will be served. She will need to file a response. After that, there will be an arraignment where your daughter can enter a plea."

Sofia nodded but could barely breathe. After the police officers left, Vanessa wanted to go to her room and Sofia let her go. On automatic pilot, she slid the yeast rolls into the oven and stirred the minestrone, but she'd lost all appetite for it. Part of her was upset with Jim. Why hadn't he thought to check attendance records for Vanessa too and forewarn her?

She collapsed onto a kitchen stool. To be fair, it had probably never entered Jim's mind that Vanessa had actually skipped school and lied about it. Sofia didn't want to believe it either.

Sofia couldn't blame the police for charging Vanessa, but her mother's heart knew they were wrong. She had to prove it somehow, but could she do it alone?

Chawton Village, England
July 1812

Jane yearned for some time alone after church, but Mamma wouldn't let the fiasco rest. With every retelling of Jane bursting into the church, it got more dramatic.

"Mamma," Cassandra finally protested, "Jane did *not* yell that a murderer was on the loose or that we were all about to have our throats slit."

Sitting by the window, Jane mouthed a silent thank-you to her sister for the effort, but she knew nothing would divert Mamma until she'd thoroughly worn herself out with the drama. "Save your breath to cool your porridge, Mamma," she muttered under her breath.

Jane had given up defending herself or correcting her mother's version. Instead, she bent over a square of linen on which she was designing a pattern for Anne Powell's wedding handkerchief. Turning her chair slightly to keep up with the movement of the sun, she concentrated on the floral border design. When she got Anne's approval, she'd replicate the design on the silk.

Except for it being hard on her eyes, Jane loved doing white-work embroidery. The baby's-breath design would be a lovely complement to Anne's gown. If she had more time, the design would look stunning on Anne's veil too. That was what she'd always imagined for her own bridal gown . . . if she'd ever married. Now, though, her imagined nuptials were all for Lizzie Bennet.

Indistinct voices from the lane grew louder as the returning picnickers got closer and children raced past Chawton Cottage. That was one thing about living in a former inn set at the crossroads of the two main thoroughfares in the area: Not many people could come or go without passing right under the Austen ladies' noses if they were curious enough to watch out the window all day.

Jane pulled back from the sitting room window as three families strolled by. She didn't want them to think she'd been watching for their return. The women carried sleeping babies, food baskets, and blankets. Jane expected that a good time was had by all—by all but the Austens, anyway.

Jane watched as the families across the lane disappeared indoors and then reappeared without the dozing babies. Chairs were brought outside, followed by women carrying sewing baskets. Groups of three or four sat in front gardens, each woman with sewing in her lap, to capture the day's remaining sunshine.

Like most families in Chawton, the Austens burned perhaps one candle at night, but it wasn't bright enough for reading or sewing. As Mamma said, when the sun went down, it was the good Lord's hint that it was time for bed. Jane shook her head, pitying the women for their inordinate amount of mending, even on a Sunday. *Children must spend every waking moment shredding their clothes,* she thought.

But when she stopped to stretch her stiff neck half an hour later, she looked more closely. That wasn't *mending* the ladies on the opposite corner were bent over. The cloth was too brightly colored for that. Where had they found *new* cloth?

"Cassandra, come look." Jane pulled back the drape. "The shop must have received another delivery recently."

Cassandra shrugged. "Perhaps, but they've sewn like that for weeks. Did you never notice?"

Jane shook her head. The side garden across the lane wasn't visible from the dining parlor where she wrote or played the pianoforte, nor from her upstairs bedchamber that faced the back courtyard.

"How can they afford to buy new cloth?" Jane mused. "They don't dress in new clothes. If they are selling finished garments, who can be buying them?" England had always relied on European markets to buy their clothing, but for many years, trading with Europe had been cut off by the war.

Cassandra shrugged. "God provides," she said simply.

Mamma bustled over to the window and budged Jane aside to peer out. "I'll run over there for a moment," she said, "and see how the picnic was that we weren't invited to." She glared pointedly at Jane.

"That truly isn't my fault," Jane protested.

But Mamma had already grabbed her sewing basket and now marched with purpose across the lane.

Cassandra closed the door behind her. "Quickly, Jane, before Mamma returns," she said. "Tell me anything you left out."

Jane smiled, acknowledging their lifelong habit of editing their words around Mamma. Their mother could blow even the smallest trouble all out of proportion.

"Mamma missed her calling when she didn't go on the stage," Jane said. Then she filled Cassandra in on the details of the person she'd seen going in and out of the neighbors' cottages. "He was a giant. No one from the village, I'm sure of it. And no matter what the men said, their front doors weren't locked." Jane paced back and forth across the sitting room while her sister kept watch at the window. "And another thing. I've been thinking about Anne Powell's gift of silk and lace, plus the fact that the Powells had plenty of coal to warm their house, and brandy to share with Mamma. And Mrs. Powell wore new shoes. Leather."

"Leather?" Cassandra whipped around, all astonishment. "That cannot be. Perhaps they were cleverly patched—"

"No, they were new. Both shoes still looked identical." Jane frowned and rubbed her tired eyes. "Something very peculiar is afoot in—"

"Jane, shhh."

The door to the sitting room banged open, and Mamma bustled in. "Those midges." She waved her hand before her face as if the swarm had followed her home. "I don't know how the neighbors can bear to sit outside on damp summer evenings and be eaten alive." She scratched at her neck and lower arms where the skin was exposed.

Jane bit her tongue. There was no point in reminding her for the hundredth time that one had to cover up at dawn and dusk on damp or cloudy summer days or the swarms of midges would bite. While they didn't transmit disease, thank heavens, their bites could still be painful, itch intensely, and make a person swell up alarmingly.

Jane folded her practice embroidery design and tucked it away. "I'll play, shall I?"

"Please do," Cassandra said. With any luck, Jane's music would calm Mamma and drown out her complaints.

Jane escaped across the hall to the dining parlor, where the pianoforte's music was spread out and waiting. It was as good an instrument as could be had for thirty guineas. She ran her hands lightly over the keys. Should she play a sonata or a reel? Jane flexed her fingers, which felt exceedingly stiff tonight. Dampness in the air bothered her more of late.

She finally settled on several pieces, including her favorites, "Bessy Bell and Mary Gray" and "The Last Time I Came o'er the Moor." As she warmed up by playing scales, Jane heard Mamma tell Cassandra that the neighbors were saving the garments they sewed to sell after the war when trade embargoes would be lifted. Jane frowned. How could they afford to tie up money buying material with perhaps no sales for years?

"I don't understand how they always beat us to the shop." Mamma's peevish voice carried. "We couldn't buy material for the new bed quilt and had to use linings of old dresses."

"I imagine they saved it from more-prosperous days," Cassandra said, her gentle voice soothing Mamma like no one else in the family could.

Jane didn't know what to believe. The day had sparked more questions than answers. And something warned her that it was only the beginning.

Jane finished both long pieces and reached for a third one. Before she could strike the first chord, Mamma called out from the sitting room.

"Jane, come here and entertain us," she cried.

"What," Jane said under her breath, "do you think I have been doing in here?" But she called out, "Yes, Mamma. Shall I read *Fordyce's Sermons* to you?"

"No," Cassandra called back. "Please read to us from *First Impressions*."

"She means *Pride and Prejudice*," Mamma corrected, "or whatever you're calling the story this year."

Jane winced at that comment. It was true that her manuscript had changed titles over the years. Even Jane could hardly believe that she'd been working with Lizzie and Mr. Darcy for sixteen years. It was true that her story hadn't found a welcome reception in the publishing world when she'd submitted it years ago.

Surely she would meet with success this time.

7

Cabot Falls, Vermont
Present Day

After a tense supper, Jim motioned to Vanessa. "It's time we talked."

Sofia removed the soup tureen and told the other children to go do homework.

"Can we stick around and listen if we don't interrupt?" Matthew asked.

Luke grabbed Matthew's sleeve. "Come on. Leave them alone."

Sofia smiled at him, grateful at how compassionate Luke had been since learning about Vanessa's brush with the law. Instead of teasing and heckling her, they seemed to have closed ranks against this attack from the outside world.

Jim pushed aside the basket of leftover rolls and leaned over the table. "Vanessa, it's important that you open up to us. You're facing serious charges, not only for skipping school, but for what witnesses say occurred while you had Mom's car."

Vanessa stared at her lap and seemed to shrink. Sofia's heart ached for her, but this had to be dealt with.

"Well?" Jim asked. "You claimed that someone could vouch for you not being at the address where the child was almost hit. It's time to tell us who that friend is."

"I can't." Vanessa looked from her dad to her mom and back to her dad. "I wasn't there. I promise. You know I'd never leave the scene of an accident. You should believe me."

"We do believe you," Jim said, "but that won't be enough for the police. I understand that your license will be revoked. Also you're to report to the principal's office in the morning about skipping. You'll get detention, I should think."

Sofia laid her hand on Vanessa's. "Why can't you tell us where you were yesterday? Did you go out of town? Is that it?" She was strictly forbidden to drive on the highway alone.

Vanessa stared in silence at her bowl of minestrone, still nearly full but now grown cold.

Jim pushed back his chair. "Think about what you're doing, honey. The sooner you come clean, the better. And until you do, you're grounded."

"Can I go now?"

Jim hesitated, then gave a quick nod. Sofia waited until Vanessa's footsteps faded away in the upper hall. "What are we going to do?" she asked.

"I don't know," Jim sighed. "Right now, I'll be happy if we don't get sued."

While loading the dishwasher together, there was a huge thump overhead from the boys' room. Jim gave Sofia a hug. "I'd better go see what the young bucks are doing."

Sofia started the dishwasher and then stared out the kitchen window. Sofia knew that she couldn't sit and do nothing. If Vanessa wouldn't talk, Sofia would dig around on her own. They needed some answers—and soon.

After wiping off the counters and degreasing the stove top, Sofia zipped on her jacket and headed outside to her car parked in the driveway. The mini LED flashlight she grabbed helped illuminate the dimly lit corners of the Suburban that the vehicle's interior lights didn't reach.

For ten minutes she searched the glove compartment, floors,

garbage bags, cup holders, and under the floor mats. She wasn't looking for anything specific, just a clue to where Vanessa had gone when she should have been in school.

"What's up?" a chipper voice asked.

Sofia jerked around, hitting her head on the door. "Oh . . . hi, Pat." She stood up, massaging her temple and then rubbing her cold hands together.

"Lose something?"

"No." She met the elderly teacher's inquisitive gaze, recognizing that nosy look from years ago when she'd been passing notes in high school English. It was still awkward for Sofia to call her anything but Mrs. Cooper.

"I couldn't help noticing the police were here twice," Pat said. "Ryan Quimby wouldn't tell me anything. Is there any way I can help?"

Embarrassment washed over Sofia, but she swallowed her pride and filled her neighbor in on what had happened. "We've reached a stalemate with Vanessa."

"I remember how hard spring was," Pat said. "The students turned into wild young colts, kicking up their heels, straining at the rules. It's very common."

"I suppose," Sofia said, "but it isn't common for Vanessa."

"I'll help you look for clues." Pat flexed her biceps. "In all the cop shows, they hunt under the seats for objects dropped by the perp."

Sofia stifled a laugh. Pat fancied herself a cross between a private eye and a crime scene investigator. "Sure. You check the backseat cushions, and I'll check the front."

Five minutes later, after finding cough drops, two dimes, a nickel, and a broken plastic spoon, Sofia's fingers closed over something small and cylindrical. She worked it out and shone her flashlight on it. An orange plastic lighter.

"Look at this." She handed it to Pat. "None of us smoke, and the kids know they aren't allowed to carry lighters."

"Do you use them to light the fireplace or candles?"

"No, we use a long-nosed disposable lighter."

Pat pursed her lips. "Kids do play with fire sometimes."

"Yes, the boys like to poke in the flames in the fireplace," Sofia said slowly. "But I don't recall ever seeing a lighter in the house. It must have fallen out of someone's pocket."

"Do any of Vanessa's friends smoke?"

"I don't think so, but I'll find out. Thanks for suggesting searching the seats." She bid Pat a good night and then turned the lighter in her hand as she watched the retired teacher head home.

Sofia shivered violently, partly from the cold and partly from the confrontation she knew was coming.

Chawton Village, England
July 1812

"Coming, Mamma." Jane jerked the sticking drawer where she kept paper and ink. "What part of *Pride and Prejudice* do you wish to hear again?"

Although her eyes were tired, Jane loved being asked to read from her own work. Cassandra was an especially loyal fan. It rallied Jane's spirits to have at least one reader intrigued by her story as the years rolled by without another sale.

Reading to Cassandra and Mamma helped pass the time as they mended household garments and pieced quilts. They pushed their chairs closer to the light of the fireplace, and Jane held her handwritten pages nearer the candle.

"I reworked the scene where Mr. Darcy proposes the first time," Jane said. "I'll read you that section and Lizzy's reply." She cleared her throat.

*"In vain have I struggled. It will not do. My feelings
will not be repressed. You must allow me to tell you how
ardently I admire and love you."*

"Oh, very nice, Jane!" Mamma interrupted. "That will melt
young Lizzie's heart."

"Perhaps not," Jane said, "as you will see."

*Elizabeth's astonishment was beyond expression.
She stared, coloured, doubted, and was silent . . . His
sense of her inferiority—of its being a degradation—of
the family obstacles . . . were dwelt on . . . He spoke of
apprehension and anxiety, but his countenance expressed
real security . . . and, when he ceased, the colour rose
into her cheeks, and she said:*

*"If I could feel gratitude, I would now thank you.
But I cannot—I have never desired your good opinion,
and you have certainly bestowed it most unwillingly."*

"Oh, poor Mr. Darcy!" Cassandra exclaimed. "My heart
breaks for him."

Jane gritted her teeth. How she hated to be interrupted in the
middle of dramatic passages. She retreated a line.

*"I have never desired your good opinion, and you
have certainly bestowed it most unwillingly."*

Cassandra leaned close. "What does Mr. Darcy say to *that*?"

"Listen," Jane replied.

*"And this is all the reply which I am to have the
honour of expecting! I might, perhaps, wish to be*

*informed why, with so little endeavour at civility, I am
thus rejected . . ."*

"*I might as well inquire,*" *replied she,* "*why with so
evident a desire of offending and insulting me, you chose
to tell me that you liked me against your will, against
your reason, and even against your character?*"

Both Cassandra and Mamma had stopped sewing, their
hands motionless in their laps. Cassandra looked astonished
at the strong language, but Mamma appeared horrified. Before
they could interrupt, Jane hurried on, feeling her own heart beat
faster as Lizzie and Mr. Darcy did verbal battle. She finished with
Elizabeth's strongest speech yet.

*"You could not have made the offer of your hand in
any possible way that would have tempted me to accept
it . . . I had not known you a month before I felt that
you were the last man in the world whom I could ever
be prevailed on to marry."*

"Oh, Jane!" Mamma cried. "You must throw that scene out
entirely. Lizzie will never get a husband, talking to men like
that. And she's throwing away Mr. Darcy and his ten thousand
pounds a year!"

Jane was not surprised by her mother's reaction, but she knew
Cassandra would give a different opinion. She waited.

Cassandra smiled tentatively. "That is very strong writing,
Jane." She hesitated.

"But?" Jane prodded.

"I agree that Lizzie shouldn't marry where she feels no love
or respect . . ."

Jane's heart sank. "But you don't like the scene, do you?"

"She is absolutely right to turn him down," Cassandra hastened to say. "I only wondered . . . I thought perhaps . . . a softer touch? Less strident and more persuasive language? You must remember her situation with her papa's estate going to his nephew after his death. She won't have a home when her parents die unless she marries."

"Exactly," Mamma said, her head bobbing. "She dare not burn her bridges with Mr. Darcy, not without other prospects. It costs a woman nothing to flatter."

"Yes, it does, Mamma. It would be a deception for Lizzie to flatter Mr. Darcy and pretend that even if he corrected his arrogance, she would marry him." Jane waved the pages through the air. "At this point, she truly has no intention of ever speaking to him again, much less marrying him."

"Jane, you take delight in vexing me!" Mamma's strident voice bordered on being shrill. "Let me remind you that you owe it to us to write something that will sell. No publisher will buy a book whose heroine offends rich men wherever she goes."

"If I can't write what I truly feel, I would rather give it up," Jane said.

"Well, you can't. You must sell. Oh, how can you be so tiresome?" Mamma took a deep breath. "Jane, remember that Cassandra and I carry the heaviest loads here. While you are whiling away the hours in the dining parlor, writing at your little desk, we are baking and gardening and growing the vegetables and sewing and cleaning—"

"With Eliza's help," Jane interrupted. She knew their maid carried the heaviest load—up before any of them each morning, lighting fires, serving breakfast, cleaning their bedchambers, and cooking.

"Jane works every bit as hard as we do, writing in the mornings," Cassandra added. "And she always helps with the cottage work after that."

"That may be true," Mamma said grudgingly, "but since she has refused to marry—refused to set up housekeeping in a great house that would have kept us all for life—then she owes it to us to write something with all that paper and ink that will make some money."

Jane's face grew warmer and warmer, and it wasn't from the dying fire. Mamma was still rankled over Jane's very short, one-day engagement to Harris Bigg-Wither nearly ten years ago. Mamma always said that a single man in possession of a good fortune must be in want of a wife. His proposal had taken Jane by surprise, and she'd been shocked into accepting. But overnight, she had come to her senses, and she had declined the following morning. It would have been a fine, big house with many servants, but like Elizabeth Bennet, Jane would not marry where there was not love.

Jane glanced at Cassandra, startled at the tears in her eyes. Cassandra hated strife, and she was also probably remembering her own fiancé, Tom Fowle, the young army chaplain who had died in 1797 from yellow fever in the Caribbean. Cassandra would have married if fate had given her a chance. And it definitely would have been for love.

Even in July, the cottage remained cool after the sun went down. As the fire burned low, when nothing was left but glowing coals, quiet settled both inside and out. The neighbors would have gone in when darkness fell, and horses and donkeys would have been bedded down with hay and straw some time ago.

Jane was deep in thought when she gradually became aware of increased noise in the lane outside: horses and carts, a wagon rumbling by, and neighbors calling to each other. Suddenly men were shouting. Jane and Cassandra sprang from their chairs simultaneously.

Mamma flew to the window, but Jane and Cassandra ran

outdoors. At the end of the lane near the doctor's cottage—called the surgery—a small crowd had gathered around a farm wagon. Jane and her sister ran down the lane to the surgery as a woman released a long, wailing scream.

8

Cabot Falls, Vermont
Present Day

Sofia slammed the car door and hurried indoors. Ten minutes later, she and Jim confronted Vanessa with the orange disposable lighter.

Vanessa's surprise seemed genuine. "It's not mine," she said. "I've never seen it before."

"Have any of your friends taken up smoking?" Sofia asked.

"No. It's a stinky habit." She wrinkled her nose. "It gets in your hair and your clothes."

And your car. Sofia hadn't noticed any smoky smell in the car. Still, the lighter had gotten there somehow, sometime.

The next morning, Sofia read a text from Julie: "Can you meet Marla and me at the chamber office at eleven and then do lunch afterward?"

She dialed Julie's number. "What's up?" she asked, afraid that she already knew.

"It's a fact-finding meeting," Julie assured her, "but if we wait to express our interest in taking over the shop's lease, we'll lose our chance."

"Have we decided that we *are* interested?"

"Interested, yes. Committed to anything, no." Someone in the background called Julie's name. "I've got to go, but can you meet us there?"

"Eleven, right?"

"Yes, and then we'll do lunch and discuss what we find out."

"Sure." Sofia realized her voice sounded flat, and she forced some enthusiasm into it. "It would be a great opportunity." *For someone,* she added silently.

What they discovered during their short meeting at the chamber-of-commerce office was that the rent would be high (no surprise), that there were strict requirements for renting on Cabot Falls historic town square (also no surprise), and that another company—Sadie's Scented Candles—had expressed an interest in the shop lease as well.

The last bit of information pushed Julie from excited to agitated. She could hardly contain herself during a lunch she barely touched.

"This is our chance, girls," she said, pushing aside her club sandwich.

"It does sound exciting." Marla removed the top slice of bread from her sandwich. "If it took off, I might even retire from the library and work in the shop full time."

"Think of the flexibility you'd have," Julie added. "No more being chained to your desk." She waited. "You're awfully quiet, Sofia. Having reservations?"

"I don't honestly know what it is." Sofia didn't want to let her friends down, but something about opening a shop didn't feel right to her. Maybe it was the cost. Her family wasn't in a position to pay rent on a shop, not on Jim's teaching salary. Or maybe her unease stemmed from her preoccupation with Vanessa's troubles.

Marla wiped her lips on a napkin. "Don't be offended by what I'm about to say, but if it's the money, we could pick up your share of the rent until you make enough sales."

"Oh, no, I couldn't let you do that."

Julie tapped her beautifully manicured nails on the edge of her plate. "You could pay us back later if you felt strongly about it."

"But pay you back out of what?" Sofia asked. A cake or pie here or there would only bring in peanuts. She needed big catering jobs or a whole tearoom to make it pay.

Julie's eyes lit up. "Remember we talked about you doing caricatures of people out on the sidewalk during good weather? It would lure people into the store, and you'd also sell them your caricatures."

"Oh, I don't know."

"Or how about this?" Marla asked. "Vanessa said her friends liked your drawings. You have a degree in studio art, so you could teach art classes in a corner of the shop. You know, something popular with kids, like cartooning or anime. Parents could shop in the store while the kids were occupied." Marla took a sip of water. "We know how busy you are with your family and Wynter's hearing issues. Julie and I have had more free time to produce paintings and crafts to sell." She laughed then. "My son's all set to empty the spare room housing my art projects and turn it into a music room."

"I admit we could use the money," Sofia said slowly. "And it's true, drawing the caricatures was quick and easy." She gazed from one dear friend to the other. "I especially don't want to keep you from getting the shop."

Sofia understood the excitement on her friends' faces. It was how she felt about her fledgling catering business. But how could she tell such good friends that she hated the idea of sketching people on the sidewalk or teaching classes in the shop?

It left her absolutely cold.

Chawton Village, England
July 1812

Jane gasped at the sound of a second chilling scream. She reached the wagon first, with Cassandra right behind, and halted abruptly. Stopped in front of the doctor's cottage surgery was a rickety cart smelling of rotted vegetables and pulled by a donkey. Several men hung about, darting furtive glances up and down the lane. Only one woman was present.

Jane leaned in, trying to see by the flickering light of a lantern held high. In the back of the cart lay two half-beaten, bleeding bodies, a boy and a man. A woman, the probable source of the scream, hugged the legs of the lanky boy and sobbed.

"Mrs. Lumb," Jane said, wrapping her arms around the short, distressed woman. Her entire body trembled, and she pressed her apron against her mouth to stifle the sobs.

"What happened to Willie and your husband?"

"I don't know!" she wailed. "My boy! And Robert!"

Jane handed Mrs. Lumb to Cassandra and then leaned over young Willie. His blackened eye was swollen shut, and his badly split lip would take time to heal. Jane pulled a linen cloth from inside her own sleeve and wiped some of the blood from Willie's face.

Jane glanced at Mr. Lumb and thought he must be dead. Eyes staring and cheeks hollow, his craggy face was covered with cuts and abrasions, and his knuckles were raw. It was obvious that he'd been on the losing end of a terrible fight. Or maybe there'd been an ambush of some kind, highwaymen that attacked both father and son. Where had they been this time of night? As head thatcher of Chawton, Robert Lumb did his work during the day. When Jane leaned over him, his hoarse whisper sounded as if a noose were tightening around his neck. She couldn't make out his muffled words.

"Move aside, move aside," Dr. Hastings commanded. The doctor was a tall, spare, beak-nosed man with an air of supreme confidence bordering on arrogance. Jane stepped out of the way while the doctor ran practiced hands over Robert Lumb's arms, chest, and torso. Then he moved over to young Willie. He had barely touched him when he muttered, "Compound fracture."

By now, several more women had joined the group, naked fear on their faces as they tried to discover who was in the wagon—and if they were alive.

"Doctor, can I help?" Jane asked. There was no nurse in the village, and the doctor had no wife to assist him.

"Do you faint over the slightest injury?" the doctor snapped.

"No, doctor, I don't," Jane said, swallowing her irritation. While Jane didn't like the sight of blood any more than the next woman, she had a strong stomach. She was nothing like Mamma, who had vapors at the most trifling invitation to drama. "So, would you like my assistance?"

"Yes, but let me move the injured inside first." He considered the dark windows of his office. "Miss Austen, find candles or lanterns to light up the operating room. Robert Lumb has deep cuts to sew, and young William has fractured his forearm." He pointed to Willie's blood-soaked sleeve where a bulge indicated the bone poking through the skin. Jane determinedly pushed down the queasiness she felt.

Dr. Hastings instructed two men to carry Robert Lumb into his surgery. Then Willie was placed on a wooden door and carried inside, his arm lying across his stomach. His face was ghostly white in the pale moonlight.

Jane clutched the doctor's sleeve, and he turned in annoyance. "What?" he snapped.

"Do you want tallow or beeswax candles? Straight or plaited wicks?"

The doctor's face registered surprise, and he acknowledged Jane's question with respect. "I need bright light, Miss Austen. White wax would be best along with the lanterns."

Jane turned to the women clustered around Mrs. Lumb and spotted the shopkeeper's wife. "Mrs. Watters, the doctor needs plenty of candles, white wax."

"I don't have plenty!" she cried. "Half a box of tallow is all. We nearly sold out the day they came in."

"Lanterns then?" Jane asked.

"None, but I'll give the doctor the candles we have. Right away." She hurried up the lane toward their shop.

The men who'd helped carry Willie and Robert inside came out and stood in an awkward huddle. Jane pushed into the center. "The doctor needs lanterns and candles. The shop doesn't have many." She turned within the circle. "Bring what you can spare."

They nodded and moved away, looking grateful for something helpful to do in the crisis. She turned back to the women, but all of them had fled except Cassandra, who still had an arm around Mrs. Lumb. "Where did they go?" Jane asked.

"They don't have much to spare, but they went home for any candle stubs they could find."

"Dr. Hastings needs whatever he can get."

A mighty yell followed by a drawn-out groan came from the doctor's surgery.

"I'd better get inside," Jane said.

Mrs. Lumb lunged away from Cassandra's supportive arm. "I'm coming too."

Jane wished she'd stay outside, but she knew that if her own loved ones were inside bleeding—maybe even dying—she'd have to be there too. "Come with her, Cassandra," Jane said. "If she faints, I won't be able to catch her." She'd cleaned wounds before for Thomas, their manservant, and it took both hands. And in the case of Willie, it might take all her strength to hold him down while the doctor set his arm and stitched up the wound.

Bobbing lights of lanterns were converging on the doctor's surgery, so Jane went inside. She followed the moaning sounds to the room near the rear of the cottage. Dr. Hastings had three candles burning and a fire roaring in the fireplace. While it felt overpoweringly hot, Jane saw the wisdom in it. Light was necessary immediately, and both injured men were shaking.

Mrs. Lumb cried out and stumbled to the table, but Cassandra pulled her back. "Shhh, Molly."

Doctor Hastings didn't look up from washing the cuts, but his voice had a steel edge to it. "You'll have to leave if you aren't quiet."

"I have to stay!" Molly Lumb cried, her voice sounding strangled. She gulped hard.

Cassandra guided her to a chair and lowered her. It had the double advantage of supporting her weak legs and preventing a bird's-eye view of the operating tables where both Robert and Willie lay trembling, their legs convulsing uncontrollably.

Jane caught Cassandra's eye. "Get some very sweet tea into her soon," she said, falling back on the traditional English remedy for shock. She raised her voice. "Doctor, the men are coming with more lanterns." As if they'd heard her, heavy footsteps sounded in the entrance hall. Jane took the lanterns and positioned them around the surgery, and each one added a measure of light until the area around the two men was like daylight. Mrs. Kearley arrived with a wicker basket of candle stubs, all sizes, and several candlesticks. Jane thanked her and then set several of them nearby, ready to light.

The doctor glanced up briefly. "Thank you for the light. I'll clean Robert's wounds, wrap them, and stitch him later." He glanced at Mrs. Lumb and lowered his voice. "I'm worried about young William. That arm needs to be set immediately. If only the village had an icehouse. I would have a better chance of saving his arm if I could get the swelling down. But first, go to my kitchen and make some sugar water for both men. It will help stop their shaking."

Jane nodded, hurried to make the sugar water, and returned to help the doctor get it into both men. Then she braced herself for what was to come.

"Doctor, will you have to amputate?" Mrs. Lumb asked, her voice so full of fear she nearly choked.

Dr. Hastings hesitated, then pulled her up from the chair and led her into the hall. Jane and Cassandra followed. "I must be frank, Mrs. Lumb," the doctor said. "His arm doesn't look good. If he were older, like your husband, I would amputate without hesitation and cauterize the stump immediately to stop infection."

Mrs. Lumb gasped but straightened her spine, eyes locked on the doctor's. "Infection? You mean gangrene?"

"Or lockjaw, which would kill him in a fortnight. Gangrene would finish him in five days once it sets in. Amputation is the best chance to save your son's life. It's your choice."

Jane shuddered. Yes, amputation would save young Willie's life, but he'd be left a cripple for the remainder of it.

"Mrs. Lumb?" the doctor asked. "You must decide now."

She swallowed hard. "Save his arm, doctor."

He nodded. Although he'd laid out the dangers, he clearly approved of her decision. Jane followed him back into the surgery room, and Cassandra guided Mrs. Lumb back to a chair. "I'll get you some more tea, Molly."

After the doctor took his position, Jane placed herself between Willie and Molly Lumb to block her view. Hearing her son's moans would be trial enough without seeing the bone protruding through his flesh.

Cassandra returned with tea, and between sips, Molly whispered, "What will we do if Robert and Willie can't work anymore?"

"Shhh," Cassandra soothed her. "They'll be thatching again in no time. Wait and see."

Jane hoped so. A master thatcher was vital to the village. Good thatch often swept down over eaves and windows, stretching toward the ground, and sometimes even covered walls.

"People aren't thatching these days," the distraught wife said. "It's too expensive. With the war, no one is building new cottages."

Jane looked over her shoulder at Cassandra and frowned. Molly was right. With a few repairs, a good thatched roof lasted about sixty years. Without new cottages, there was little work for a family thatching business such as theirs. That being true, Jane wondered, what did Molly Lumb mean about her husband and son getting back to work? What work?

"Ready, Miss Austen?" Doctor Hastings said.

Jane nodded and focused on the patient. They weren't just dealing with a severely broken arm though. Molly's heart was close to breaking too.

9

Cabot Falls, Vermont
Present Day

After the lunch meeting with her friends, Sofia needed a break from the pressure Julie and Marla were putting on her to lease a shop to sell their art. She could think of no better way to lose herself in her own creative thoughts than to work on deciphering the mystery of the third quilt square.

Before she involved Marla, who had terrific resources at the library plus a serious interest in genealogy, Sofia wanted to do some digging of her own. She realized that the chances of Jane Austen embroidering her quilt square and being related to her somehow were extremely small. Still, maybe she'd find that Jane had at some point gone to Italy.

Her first Internet search came up with thousands of links to Jane Austen all around the world. She'd had no idea there was a Jane Austen Society in the United States. But to learn about her embroidery, she needed to track down museums with virtual tours.

Soon, Sofia was happily lost in Jane Austen's world, reveling in close-ups of her home in Chawton Village in south central England. Chawton Cottage had been converted into Jane Austen's House Museum. Sofia's mouth practically watered. If she were visiting there, she could walk through the rooms where Jane had actually lived and worked. Many keepsakes of the family were on view, including her father's bookcase and a quilt made by the Austen women. There was a simple twelve-sided walnut table, barely wide enough to hold an inkwell, a quill pen, and a few sheets of paper. There Jane Austen had sat, overlooking the busy village street, transforming *First Impressions* into *Pride and Prejudice* and writing her later novels, *Mansfield Park, Emma, Northanger Abbey,* and *Persuasion.*

Sofia clicked on the link to the quilt made by the Austen ladies, but it was a disappointment. Although it was pretty enough, and understandably housed behind a glass partition, it didn't look anything like the whitework silk-and-lace square in Nonna's quilt.

"Maybe I need to be more specific," Sofia mumbled.

A search on "Jane Austen Needlework" and "Jane Austen Embroidery" hit the jackpot. The photos from museum archives that appeared on her computer screen took her breath away.

She leaned close to the screen and clicked for several close-ups. Also in the museum were a muslin handkerchief and a lawn collar, embroidered by Jane Austen in a whitework pattern very similar to the one in Nonna's quilt. From what Sofia could see so far, it was certainly possible that the "J.A." stood for "Jane Austen."

Barely breathing, Sofia went on to read how whitework embroidery was frequently used on muslin dresses, fine lawn caps, handkerchiefs, tablecloths, and bed linens. Patterns were featured in periodicals for ladies, showing many different motifs, some fancier than others.

Sofia had to tell someone. Who would appreciate the possibility—even if miniscule—that they could be related to Jane Austen? Vanessa.

Sofia carried the open laptop upstairs to the girls' bedroom and knocked on the door. Wynter was working at her desk, and Vanessa was in bed reading *Pride and Prejudice.* She appeared to be about half-done with the book.

"Can you girls promise to keep a secret?" Sofia asked. "It's not a for-sure secret, but it's an exciting possibility."

"What is it?" Wynter asked.

"You look like Matthew on Christmas morning," Vanessa added.

Sofia laughed at the apt comparison. "If this turns out to be true—and I'm a long way from knowing yet—it'll be that exciting."

She told them about the third quilt square, describing both the whitework and the signature of "In friendship, J.A." Then she turned the laptop around so they could both see the website. "Look at this. These are both pieces done by Jane Austen. J.A."

Vanessa and Wynter studied the screen.

"Mom, that's incredible." Vanessa looked up, eyes enormous. "Could we really be connected to Jane Austen somehow?" She frowned then. "Wait. The quilt was made by my great-great-grandmother in Italy, not England. Right?"

"I know. It's a long shot, but wouldn't it be something? For some reason, that white square in our Italian quilt is signed in English."

"How will you find out?" Wynter asked.

"I don't know yet. Marla is a genius at genealogy, and she'll help me. And half a dozen Austen websites have good contact information so you can ask curators questions."

"Hurry up and find out," Vanessa said. "Can you imagine Miss Jameson's face if I said I could prove we're related to Jane Austen? Imagine what your drawings would sell for then."

"I'm a long way from proving that, so mum's the word, even with your lit teacher. I don't know when—or even *if*—we could tell." She kissed them both. "Don't stay up too late now."

She closed their bedroom door, fueled by their excitement as well as her own. Even so, she had to find that direct link with Jane's embroidery. How could it have ended up in her priceless Italian quilt?

Chawton Village, England
July 1812

How could Willie have ended up in such a state? Jane wondered. She stifled her horror when the doctor exposed Willie's arm. She intentionally smiled down at Willie in what she hoped was a reassuring look, but he squeezed his eyes shut. A tear escaped and slid down the side of his temple.

"We'll set the break first," Dr. Hastings said, keeping his voice low. "I'll give the lad a bit of opium for the pain. The hardest part for William will be when I put the bone back into place. Stitching and splinting will be easier on him—and us." He smiled briefly, and Jane's heart warmed to him. Beneath his all-business exterior, he truly cared. The worry in his eyes gave him away.

While the doctor administered the painkiller, Jane lit a candle and held it high over them to brighten the immediate area. She nodded to Cassandra, who wrapped her arms around Molly Lumb. The doctor cut away the blood-soaked shirt, exposing a skinny set of ribs and arms with sinewy young muscles. Jane gulped and swallowed over and over at the white bone showing through the skin. But she held the candlestick steady.

The doctor placed a rolled piece of cloth between Willie's front teeth. "Bite down, son."

Jane was unprepared for the cracking noise as the doctor snapped the bone back into place. Willie screamed and arched his back; the tears flowed freely now, but he stifled his screams into moans as the first searing pain subsided.

Jane crouched beside Willie, careful to keep the candle upright and stay out of the doctor's way. "You're going to be fine," she whispered.

Willie turned his head from side to side and spit out the cloth. "Papa?"

"He'll be fine too," Jane assured him. "The doctor will tend to him when your arm is set." *And your swollen eye is checked and your cuts are stitched and your broken ribs wrapped*, she added silently. Jane caught a glimpse of the dark black thread attached to the doctor's curved needle before it disappeared into flesh. But the opium had enough effect that Willie could stand the stitching of his wound with only occasional moans escaping him.

Mrs. Lumb's voice was stronger now. "I'm here, Willie, right behind the doctor. I won't leave you." She sat up straighter. "You'll be fine. You'll see."

Jane kept her eyes and her smile trained on Willie's face. When her candle burned short, Cassandra appeared at her elbow with a new one, already lit, and swapped them. Two of the short candles had burned down to puddles of wax and spluttered out by the time the stitching was done and the padded splint was wrapped around Willie's arm. Jane held the two pieces in place, one inside and one outside his arm, while the doctor wrapped it in strips of cloth.

"It should be tight enough to immobilize the limb," Dr. Hastings said, "but not so tight that it restricts circulation. You only want to restrict circulation when there is profuse bleeding."

Jane nodded, but she hoped she never had need of that information again in her life. She was glad to help, truly glad, but she was also convinced that she wasn't cut out to be a surgical nurse. Writing about such trauma would be enough to satisfy her.

The doctor fetched a large square of clean, worn cloth and folded it diagonally to make a triangle. He placed the arm at a right angle across Willie's stomach, eliciting a groan, then placed the material under his arm and brought the other two ends over each shoulder. Jane lifted Willie's head so the doctor could tie the sling behind his neck.

Mrs. Lumb moved to where her husband was resting on the

next table, although how he could sleep, Jane had no idea. Surely his eyes were only closed. Molly patted his shoulder, but there was no response. She patted one leg, but still he made no sound or movement.

"Robert?" Molly whispered, shaking his shoulder this time. "Robert?" she said louder. Then she whipped around. "Doctor! He's dead!"

Moaning, Willie tried to sit up. But Jane gently forced him back down. "Stay still. I'm sure he's just asleep."

"No he isn't!" Molly dragged on the doctor's sleeve.

He leaned over Robert Lumb, then felt his neck. "Light!" he commanded.

Jane shook a finger at Willie. "Lie still." She took the candlestick to give the doctor bright light over Robert. He was certainly still.

Dr. Hastings lifted Robert's eyelids "He's had a blow to the head," the doctor said. "He was in more pain than he let on, apparently. He's passed out."

Molly's eyes grew round. "He's not dead?"

"No, he's unconscious. It's easier for the body to handle pain that way." He examined Robert's head and torso. "I see no reason for him to stay unconscious long. Let's do all we can before he wakes up."

For more than an hour, Jane and the doctor worked together, with Jane cleaning wounds and Dr. Hastings stitching where needed. Halfway through, Robert regained consciousness, to Molly's great relief and his intense discomfort. Most of the candles and stubs had burned down to nothing by the time the doctor finished, but the lanterns burned strong.

Back aching, Jane held Willie's hand until he finally dozed off from a combination of the painkiller and total exhaustion. Gently she slipped her hand out of his curled fingers. The room was darker now, as several men had returned and taken their lanterns home when the emergency passed.

Jane found Cassandra waiting for her in the sitting room with the doctor, who was finishing a cup of tea. He stood and shook Jane's hand. "Thank you for your help," he said. "You stepped forward when needed. I don't care what others say—" He stopped abruptly and gave an embarrassed cough. "You can go now. I'll stay up with the patients, and Mrs. Lumb is staying."

Jane nodded, struck by the oddity of his remark. He liked her despite what villagers were saying about her? She raised an eyebrow at Cassandra, who only shrugged and followed her into the hall.

"Did you hear how it happened?" Jane whispered. "Did anyone tell you?"

"I don't think anyone knows." Cassandra yawned. "Mamma came earlier to see what happened to us, but she didn't stay long."

Jane reached for the front door, then froze at the sound of raised voices behind them. She put a finger to her lips.

"But why can't you stop?" Molly begged. "Please, Robert. You and William could both have been killed."

"Stop it," he said, his voice rough. "Do you want to starve then?"

"No, but I don't want to be a widow and childless either."

Jane's eyes met her sister's. What was Molly begging him to stop?

Cassandra tugged on Jane's arm, and Jane reluctantly followed her out the front door. A small knot of people still stood in the front garden. Several of them melted into the night, but three remained.

One man, a spare, beak-nosed laborer with a scraggly mustache, stepped forward and blocked their way to the street. "How are Robert and Willie?" he asked, his voice gruff but his expression one of concern.

"Robert has regained consciousness," Jane said, "and he has cuts and bruises." She glanced down at the bloodstains on her white apron. "Willie's broken arm was set, and he's resting now. He is badly cut and bruised." Cassandra passed behind Jane and tugged on her hand. Jane followed briefly, then turned back. "Who found the Lumbs?" she asked.

She met nothing but blank, hostile stares.

Jane tried again, thinking she hadn't been clear. "Where were the Lumbs found tonight?"

Finally one man, the local miller, spoke up. "Johnson Road."

Jane frowned. That was several miles away, nowhere near the Lumbs' cottage. "What were they—"

"Go home." The miller, Richard Gummer, stepped toward her, glaring.

Stunned, Jane turned to leave. She'd never felt such hostility. But why? She hadn't done anything. What were the villagers hiding? Why had they banded together against the Austen women?

"What's going on?" Jane whispered, her arm tucked into Cassandra's as they hurried up the dark lane.

"Shhh." Cassandra glanced over her shoulder. "Let's talk about this inside. The night has ears."

"And very unfriendly ones," Jane added.

Jane was bone weary, partly from helping the doctor and partly from the knowledge that she had enemies. She longed for tea and cake by the fire in their safe cottage.

Jane led the way up the dark path to their front entrance. She reached for the latch at the same instant that she spied something white nailed to the door. "Cassandra, look." It was a paper. Jane pulled it loose and unfolded it.

Cassandra clutched Jane's arm. "What is it?"

"I can't make out the words." Jane carried the paper inside to the sitting room and leaned near a candle on the small side table.

Remembering the hostile neighbors, she had a sinking feeling that it was a threat. Instead, she was surprised. "Keep looking," the note read. "All is not what it seems."

10

Cabot Falls, Vermont
Present Day

After tucking the girls in, Sofia's excitement about her quilt research drained away. She had to face it. Vanessa's time was running out. She had to keep looking. But where?

Before bed, Sofia pulled the last load of laundry from the dryer. Buying Matthew washable winter jackets was the smartest thing she'd done in years. She'd never known a child who could spill more than he did. She examined his jacket—*good, no more stains*—and hung it in the coat closet. When doing so, she managed to knock Vanessa's coat to the floor. Sofia sighed. She'd swear that her kids never actually touched the coat hangers. They flung their coats at the closet.

After hanging it back up, Sofia noticed a scrap of paper on the floor. Glancing at it before throwing it away, she froze. She couldn't quite process what she was seeing.

It was a ticket stub for a movie theater. The computer-generated receipt had the name of the movie plus a date and time. Monday at 1:10 p.m. The hour when Vanessa skipped school.

So that's where Vanessa was, Sofia thought. She'd evidently slipped out to see this movie and then hurried back for her prom meeting.

Sofia stuck the ticket stub in her pocket, suddenly recalling the snippet of phone conversation she'd overheard Sunday morning.

She'd bet her bottom dollar now that Abby hadn't called to ask about transportation of their science project. No. Vanessa was talking about their movie plans when she'd said it was "all worked out."

Relief at where she'd been was mixed with suppressed fury that Vanessa hadn't told them about the movie. Skipping school was wrong, yes, but not nearly as bad as letting them wonder if she'd left the scene of an accident.

Sofia found Jim in the family room and showed him the ticket stub. "Now we know, at least. What do we do?"

He didn't answer right away. "I'm glad it was just a movie," he finally said. "But that still leaves unanswered questions."

Sofia shivered. "I think the police have all the answers they need."

Jim pulled Sofia down beside him on the couch. "Try not to get even more upset. It won't help."

"I know." Sofia agreed, but she felt she had a right to be upset. She'd had to deal with the police twice this week while Jim was at school. She remained quiet, but turmoil still brewed inside her.

Chawton Village, England
July 1812

For two days, Jane hid the turmoil inside her as she analyzed the note nailed to the door: "Keep looking. All is not what it seems." She and Cassandra had agreed to keep the note a secret from Mamma, but it was never far from Jane's thoughts.

According to the doctor, Willie Lumb was feverish, which was to be expected. Jane and Cassandra planned to visit him when he was stronger.

After lunch one day, Jane headed to the Powell cottage. She hoped Anne would be pleased with the practice design she'd worked out. She was eager to start on the actual silk square now that her revisions of *Pride and Prejudice* were finished and she was at the recopying stage.

Anne welcomed her at the door with scissors in hand, and Jane laughed. "I can guess what you're doing today."

"We just started," Anne said. "Come in."

In the dining parlor, the table had been cleared for the silk and the wedding dress pattern pieces.

"I'm so afraid of making a mistake," Mrs. Powell said. "One wrong cut could ruin this beautiful cloth."

"She's making me cut it," Anne said. "Any mistakes will be my fault." She smiled, obviously thrilled to sew the dress she'd wear to begin married life with her naval hero.

"I won't interrupt your dressmaking for long," Jane said, pulling the linen square from her skirt pocket. "I designed your handkerchief first on this." She smoothed it out on the table. "What do you think? If you like the design, I'll use it for a pattern on the silk and trim it with the lace you gave me."

"Oooh, Mamma, look," Anne said. "What intricate work."

"I've never used this particular design before," Jane said, pleased at her reaction. "It's special for you."

Mrs. Powell pointed to a blank corner. "What about this?"

"That's where I'll sign it." Jane folded it up and put it in her pocket. "I can begin the silk handkerchief without delay."

"Oh, please stay," Anne said. "For a little while?"

Jane considered how many daylight hours were left, then nodded. She could put off her copying for a bit. She looked at her ink-stained fingers with dismay though. The stains might bleed onto the silk. She rubbed her hands hard against the back of her skirt. "I can help pin patterns," she offered. "I'm quite efficient at using every scrap of cloth."

For the next hour, she helped the Powell ladies pin on various pattern pieces. Some adjustments required re-pinning, but accuracy was imperative before scissors touched the expensive fabric. As she pinned, Jane couldn't help wondering again at how it had come to be in Anne's possession.

Keep looking, the note had said.

So, Jane looked. And what she noticed made the tension mount in her by the minute.

When Jane dropped a pin on the floor and went down on hands and knees to find it, her eyes were barely inches away from Mrs. Powell's shoes. Definitely new shoes, not newly patched. New *leather* shoes. Cassandra was wrong; Jane had not imagined that. Standing again, she glanced furtively around the room at a new coat on a chair near the door, the full coal scuttle, and a box of extra candles. Only last week Mrs. Powell had given her a bottle of brandy for Mamma. Jane had heard that the only pubs still in business were selling smuggled spirits.

All is not what it seems, the note said. But what exactly?

Jane considered the secretive, frosty way the villagers had treated her lately. And the intensive sewing done by the neighbors despite material shortages and no one to buy the finished dresses. And the beatings of the Lumbs. What had they been doing out at that hour? And what did they own that anyone would bother to steal?

Jane could no longer avoid what was staring her in the face. A smuggling operation was going on right under her nose. Maybe it had been for a long time. Certainly the wars had produced poverty and shortages of all kinds.

But to be involved in smuggling? Not the village of Chawton.

"Jane, are you unwell?" Anne asked.

Startled, Jane forced a smile. "My mind wanders, I'm afraid."

She couldn't ignore where her mind had gone. The signs seemed obvious now. Anne's wedding dress was undoubtedly being made with illegally obtained goods, not some "gift" from her fiancé. How could she tell her friend? Jane hated to ruin such a joyful time, but if she didn't reveal the probable truth, someone could report Anne's family for smuggling—for being traitors.

If I figured it out, it won't be long before someone else does too. Anne's family could be hung for it. Jane shuddered, but she knew she had no alternative. She must break the news to her friend, no matter how devastating it would be.

It was nearly time for the midday meal. "Before I leave," Jane said, turning to Anne, "would you take a turn about the village with me? I feel a need for fresh air before going home."

Anne shot her a quizzical look, but she seemed to understand that Jane was asking for some privacy. "I'll be back soon, Mamma." Anne grabbed her bonnet off the hook and fairly skipped out the front door.

Jane followed at a more-sedate pace appropriate for her thirty-seven years. She linked arms with Anne and turned toward Chawton Pond. The pond was full now, and sparkly blue dragonflies and damselflies flitted over the water. Jane cleared her throat, started to speak, then cleared her throat again.

"What is it, Jane?" Anne asked. "Is there a bee in your bonnet?"

"I fear that it's true. I'm searching for the words." In silence she strolled down the lane leading to the church. It always amazed Jane how quickly muddy roads could dry and turn to dusty ones. In the shade of the gnarled yew tree, Jane put out a hand to stop Anne. "I want to talk to you . . . about the silk and lace you received."

Anne laughed out loud. "I'm all astonishment. I thought you meant to warn me that I am too young to be engaged."

"No, it's about the lace and silk. And the new shoes and coats and the brandy." She took a deep breath. "I don't believe the gifts came from your fiancé. I think you received smuggled goods."

Anne's eyes danced with merriment. "Smuggled goods?" When Jane didn't join in the laughter, the significance of her words seemed to sink in. "Are you serious?" Anne shrugged off Jane's hand. "You think my George is a smuggler? How could you say such a thing?"

"No, I don't think that. With my own two brothers in the navy, I have the highest regard for our heroes." Jane begged her silently to understand. "I don't believe that either your brother or your father picked up a package sent to you by your fiancé." Jane waited for her words to penetrate.

Confusion was slowly replaced by a dawning horror. "You're accusing my brother and father of being smugglers?" Her voice rose an octave. "That's not possible. Smugglers own ships. My father's never even been on one. And my brother's afraid of drowning."

"You're talking about sea smugglers," Jane said. "Dry-land smugglers receive the goods and bring the contraband inland."

"But all those things were gifts."

"Anne, my dear, you're being naïve. No other fighting men are sending such treasures home, including my own brothers."

"Why would they?" Anne's brows drew together in a scowl. "Your brother Edward's the squire of the village. Your navy brothers don't worry that *you'll* starve!"

Jane stepped back at the reprimand. Yes, it was true that her brother Edward had been adopted by a wealthy childless couple, the Knights of Kent, and he enjoyed the freehold of more than thirty cottages in Chawton as well as the Great House, farm, and Chawton Park. But what most people, including Anne, didn't understand was that as the heir, he was more a tenant than an owner. The upkeep of those estates took a crippling amount of resources. Also Edward's family was large. He had eleven children of his own, plus seven brothers and sisters, biological and adoptive mothers, and the Knights' extended family to care for. Jane could only imagine the pressure he was under and how thin his resources were stretched.

"Yes, we have the use of Chawton Cottage," Jane admitted, "and a small amount of yearly income." But they had to scrimp and economize far more than any of the villagers realized. Jane's writing wasn't frivolous. It needed to bring in income. "Everyone is suffering deprivation during the war, Anne, but smuggling isn't the solution. If it's true and if your brother gets caught, he'll be hanged."

Anne gasped, then pivoted on her heel and ran alone farther into the churchyard, past the rows of graves. Jane clenched her hands at her sides, yet she had to let her go. She had hit the girl with a terrible idea. It would take time to sink in. Ten minutes passed while Anne stumbled through the graveyard, head down, stopping for a moment, only to stroll on again. Finally she returned to where Jane waited by the church doors.

"Jane, I'm sorry for what I said." Anne pulled her shawl tighter despite the warmth of the day. "My George is so brave. I know he sent me that package. It's a reminder that the war will end soon, and we'll be wed."

But who will walk you down the aisle if they hang your father and brother? Jane wanted to ask but couldn't.

They walked in silence back to Anne's house, and Anne entered alone. Jane trudged on toward Chawton Cottage. When nearly there, she spotted Mr. Powell coming toward her, hot and sweaty from working an outlying farm. Or so he always claimed. She paused and waited until Anne's father drew near. A large man, he towered over Jane.

"Beautiful day to be out," she said.

"Ah, so it is. But mending stone fences is backbreaking work."

"But it keeps the sheep at home," Jane said.

"That it does. We're shearing tomorrow. Hot work, but we're glad to see some wool, even if we use it ourselves." He wiped his face with a damp kerchief.

Jane frowned as if puzzled. "No one to buy the wool?"

"No. It's this war, Miss Austen, this war. There's no market."

Jane stepped closer, despite his overpowering smell of sweat, so her voice wouldn't carry down the lane. "If there's no market for your wool, how is it that you have new coats and boots—*leather* boots—for your family? And brandy and enough cash for coal to keep your house warm?"

Mr. Powell squinted at Jane, and his lip curled. "What are you saying?"

"I think the coats and boots and coal—and the silk and lace—were smuggled in. I think you and your son are land smugglers or you're trading with land smugglers."

"How dare you." His hand came up swiftly.

Jane jumped back out of reach. "Do you deny it?" she asked. "Or should I ask our neighbors how you came upon this sudden wealth?"

"You know nothing," Mr. Powell growled.

"If you won't talk to me, I'll find the truth another way."

The silence thickened as the sun beat down, and Jane prepared to run.

Mr. Powell's face was so red that it was nearly purple. He held his arms stiff at his sides, as if it were a strain not to hit her.

She waited.

His words were defiant when he did speak. "All right. I've done a bit of smuggling."

Jane's shock was deep. Her friend's father was a smuggler, and he didn't seem at all sorry about it. "How can you trade with our enemies?" she asked. "Anne's own fiancé and many other villagers, including my two brothers, are fighting the French and the Americans as well as violent smuggling gangs and pirates on the open seas. Yet, you're trading with the very people who want to kill Anne's fiancé and my brothers."

Mr. Powell still looked angry, but fear was mixed with it now. *But not guilt*, Jane thought.

"I only wanted Anne to have a nice wedding when the war ended."

"That isn't all you smuggled," Jane said, feeling anger rise to replace her fear. "What about the leather shoes and coats? The brandy?"

Mr. Powell stepped close, fast on his feet for such a big man, and he grabbed Jane's arm. "Don't forget the food," he said, tightening his grip, "including some on your own table."

"What do you mean?" Jane said, outraged. "We don't smuggle."

"The ham and bacon last week? The bottle of brandy Mrs. Powell gave you?" He snorted, and sweat dripped off his chin. "When you turn me in, explain that to the constable."

Jane went slack as the fight drained out of her. Could that be true? Did some of their food, the food she'd eaten and appreciated, come from smugglers? She suddenly felt faint in the heat of the noonday sun.

Was her own family involved in smuggling? *Have I been as blind as Anne?*

11

Cabot Falls, Vermont
Present Day

How could Jim be so blind to the danger to our family? Sofia asked herself over and over that night. She barely slept, other than short naps every few hours. She prayed throughout the night and tried not to resent Jim's deep, even breathing.

After everyone was delivered to school the next morning, Sofia brought her coffee to the living room, where she wrote down everything she knew, everything she suspected, and the questions the police had asked. Then she brainstormed ways to find the answers. While she'd agreed not to confront Vanessa yet, she had to do something.

Sofia decided to start at the scene of Vanessa's crime: the theater.

At the theater after lunch, she explained to the young blond ticket taker that she wasn't there to see a movie but needed information. The girl hesitated, then picked up a phone. A moment later she nodded and pointed. "Around that corner you'll find the manager's office."

It took less than five minutes for Sofia to discover that the manager couldn't help.

"There's really no way to determine if your daughter stayed through the whole movie or not," he said, straightening his tie with its theater logo. "I don't have ushers stay throughout a movie, except for a few Saturday matinees when I need a referee." He grinned at his own feeble joke. "You might ask Janeen, though, the ticket girl. She was working Monday."

Sofia thanked him for his time, walked past the concession stand with its candy and buttered popcorn and soft pretzel breadsticks, and went back to the ticket booth. She got in line behind two gray-haired ladies who were discussing the Maggie Smith movie they were about to see.

"Are you Janeen?" Sofia asked the girl when it was her turn. "Your boss said maybe you could help me. It's about someone who was here Monday."

The girl frowned in concentration. "I'll try."

Sofia pointed to a movie poster behind her. "My high school daughter was here with a friend to see that movie on Monday at one ten. Do you know Vanessa Parker?"

Janeen shook her head. "No, but if you tell me what she looks like, I might remember her. There weren't many kids here in the afternoon because of school."

Sofia grimaced. "That's where Vanessa should have been too." She rummaged in her purse for her wallet where she carried the kids' most recent school pictures. She showed the girl Vanessa's. "Do you recognize her?"

"Oh, yes," Janeen said, smiling. She looked pleased to be able to help. "She was here with another girl."

Sofia hesitated. Was someone this young reliable enough to be a police witness? "I don't want to seem nosy," she said, "but you look young enough to be in school yourself."

"I *am* in high school." Janeen pointed at her theater badge. "See this symbol at the bottom? It means I'm a work-study student. I'm studying business courses at the high school, and working here is part of that. I get credit for it, and they pay me a little besides."

"I see. That sounds like valuable experience." Sofia tried to frame her next question in a nonsuspicious way, but she couldn't.

"Can you tell me if my daughter stayed for the whole two hours of the movie?"

Janeen pressed her lips together, looked down, and squinted. "Let me think." Finally she shook her head. "I can't say for sure. I didn't see them come out when it was over, but I was busy selling tickets for the next showing."

"What do you do when you're not selling tickets?" Sofia asked. "Would you have seen her if she left for a short while?"

"I might have if it was a slow period. Lots of times there's not much to do but clean the lobby area." She tightened her ponytail. "Sometimes I get busy at the concession stand though. Then I get an usher to help me if he's done picking up trash."

"So you're saying if Vanessa and her friend left early, you might not have seen them?"

Janeen nodded slowly. "I'm afraid so."

After Sofia thanked her and left, she sat in the theater parking lot for five minutes without turning on the car. She read a text from Julie, asking if she was ready to sign on the dotted line yet for the shop in the town square. She tossed her phone into her purse. She couldn't think about that now.

Instead, Sofia studied her notebook of questions. Her gaze kept returning to the address of the curb jumping—618 Juniper Road. She'd mapped it at home. That street was only four blocks away, if she remembered right, although it was the opposite direction from the school. Vanessa would have had no reason to go that way.

No reason that Sofia knew of, anyway.

Chawton Village, England
July 1812

"No!" Jane cried, jerking her arm free from Mr. Powell's grip. She darted around him and raced home as fast as her long skirts would allow. It couldn't be true. There was no way that the mother and sister of the Squire of Chawton would be involved in smuggling.

Jane was winded by the time she arrived home. She burst through the front door. "Cassandra! Mamma!" She tugged at her bonnet strings and called again. "Cassandra! Mamma! Where are you?"

"Goodness, Jane, what's wrong?" Mamma called from the sitting room. "Is there a fire?"

"No, something infinitely worse," Jane said grimly. "Where's Cassandra?" She stood at the foot of the narrow stairs leading up to the bedchambers. "Cassandra!" she shouted again.

"Stop that caterwauling this instant. Cassandra's out in the bakehouse and can't hear you."

Jane didn't respond. Instead, she strode through the sitting room and kitchen, past the terrified-looking young Eliza, and out the side door. She stormed straight to the bakehouse with barely a glance at the kitchen garden, the paddock for the donkey, the granary, and the covered well. Even though the bakehouse door was braced open by a heavy crock, the heat from the room slammed into Jane with force. Jane tripped over the stoneware and fell, catching herself but scraping the palms of her hands.

Cassandra whipped around, her hands holding dripping clothes from the washtub. "Jane, what in the world?"

Mamma had come running as well, huffing and puffing and leaning heavily on the doorframe of the bakehouse.

"Oh, Cassandra, please tell me it's a lie," Jane said, wiping her bleeding hand on a rag. "Tell me it's not true."

"What's not true?" Her sister took the rag and got it wet.

"Is it true—could there possibly be *any* truth in Mr. Powell's accusations?" Jane swung her accusing glare from her sister to her mother. "Have you two been part of the smuggling ring in Chawton?"

The collective gasp of her mother and sister was followed immediately by Mamma swaying and threatening to collapse. Jane caught her and braced her up. "Do *not* faint, Mamma," Jane ordered.

Mrs. Austen's eyes snapped open, startled enough at Jane's unheard-of tone of voice to obey.

"Come outside," Jane said. "It's too hot in here with the fire going."

Jane led them through the graveled courtyard over to a bench and a chair in the garden under a beech tree. Bees foraged among the blue-flowered herbs and the russet-red wallflowers while the butterflies fluttered around the pale blossoms of the pinks and lavender. Cassandra and Mamma shared the bench facing Jane and waited, hands folded in their laps.

Jane took a deep breath, the peace in the garden filling her. "Let me start again. I'm sorry I shouted at you, Mamma. I've had the most distressing news, and the telling of it cannot be delayed." She forced herself to smile. "I realize now that there must be a mistake. Mr. Powell was angry when he made these wild accusations."

"About *smuggling*?" Cassandra asked, clearly confused.

Jane nodded. "He said that you had received smuggled ham and bacon and brandy. Is that true?" Jane could remember having ham several times in the past month, and she herself had brought home the bottle of brandy as a gift from Mrs. Powell to Mamma.

Cassandra glanced at Mamma, and Jane watched them both closely. While Cassandra seemed puzzled, Mamma looked frightened.

"What is it, Mamma?"

"Smuggling is illegal, Jane."

"Yes, Mamma. That's why his accusation upset me so much. But is it true?"

"Of course not, Jane," Cassandra said. "You're frightening Mamma."

Jane breathed deeply of the lavender, willing herself to remain calm. "I've been wrapped up in my writing for months," she admitted, "and I've been so grateful to you both for helping Eliza with the cooking. I do remember having pork chops and ham a few times, even bacon. Did Eliza buy it at the shop, as I always assumed?"

Mrs. Austen frowned. "Let me think." She lifted her apron and let it float down. "I remember. One Sunday before church, young Willie Lumb came to the kitchen with some ham for the larder. They'd butchered and couldn't eat it all and had no way to store the rest in this heat."

Cassandra nodded. "No one has enough salt or sugar to cure ham these days." She smiled then, at peace again. "I knew there was a simple explanation."

"It would be," Jane agreed, "if the Lumbs raised hogs. I'm quite sure they don't. Besides, the ham we ate was cured. Someone, somewhere, had preserved it."

Jane slumped back in her chair. Had she really been so buried in her writing all these months that she was oblivious to the conditions in her own home? As long as food was on the table at noon when she stopped writing, she ate it without thinking. She could understand Mamma being naïve about it, but surely Cassandra would have known something was amiss. How many other "gifts" like the ham and brandy had Mamma and Cassandra accepted?

Ignorance of receiving smuggled goods would never stand up as a defense in a court of law. The judge wouldn't believe that in these times of war and privation, anyone would believe that these were simple gifts. It was tantamount to believing in magic.

Cassandra reached over and patted Jane's knee, bringing her out of her reverie. "Do you really believe those gifts to us were smuggled in by our neighbors?"

Jane nodded slowly. "Not only that, I think Anne's gift of lace and satin for her wedding gown was smuggled in by her father as well. I expect he's selling smuggled goods to those who can pay, then using the money to buy coal. Their scuttle was full, and the fire blazed."

"But why, Jane?" Mamma asked. "Things are not so bad as that, are they?"

"For some of our neighbors, it's that bad," Jane admitted. "Not everyone has a rent-free cottage like we do from Edward. Several years ago, Frank talked of villages that were surviving the war by dealing with smugglers. But I never expected it of the people of Chawton."

Cassandra frowned. "But our neighbors don't have enough money to buy smuggled goods."

"According to Frank, some villages pool money to buy goods from smugglers. Others sell clothing to France through the smugglers. That lets them avoid British taxes, which are very heavy in the best of times."

"But we didn't know the meat and brandy were smuggled!" Mrs. Austen cried.

Cassandra wrung her hands. "Being unaware of it wouldn't stop us from being arrested, would it?"

Jane didn't answer. She didn't want to pick her mother up from one more swoon.

Jane spent the next two hours calling on neighbors and asking subtle but nosy questions. By studying their sitting rooms and parlors and dining tables, she became astute at telling which families were probably prospering from smuggling and which weren't. A few families, mostly spinsters and widows, were profuse in their praise of the neighbors who shared with them in these desperately hard times of war.

"We would have starved these last two years without them," one bedridden widow said.

In each case, Jane only smiled. She didn't have the heart to reveal where their bounty had really come from. And in truth, the neighbors had been generous with them. They could have kept all the smuggled goods themselves or sold them to people in surrounding towns for a tidy profit.

The families with men and boys who clearly were involved in the smuggling were less welcoming. One man bodily escorted Jane right back out the door. But when several of them realized that Jane had figured out their scheme, that she could name names like the Powells, they stopped pretending. Two families openly admitted it, adding names of farm laborers who smuggled too. They warned that Jane's family was in serious trouble if she let the cat out of the bag.

Finally Jane headed home, dispirited but much less confused. Smuggling was illegal, yet it appeared that the town of Chawton had been surviving the Napoleonic Wars by helping smuggle goods from the southern coastal town of Southampton. These dry-land smugglers, as her neighbors were called, brought contraband north, in some cases all the way to London. Luxury goods like brandy and cigars traveled to London on the Gosport Road that passed right by Chawton Cottage. Despite their reasons, the fact remained: Trading with the enemy was illegal.

Late that afternoon, Jane paid a visit to the Lumb family. Thatch overhung their porch, and it smelled rank. The door opened a few inches. "Hello, Molly," Jane said. "I've come to inquire after Willie and Mr. Lumb."

Reluctantly, Mrs. Lumb stood aside so Jane could enter. Their cottage was cramped, cluttered, and without many creature comforts. Two small rooms and a scullery were below. A bare wooden staircase led up to no more than two bedchambers, Jane guessed.

Mrs. Lumb pointed to the room on the left. "We moved a bed for Willie in here."

Jane fixed a smile on her face and was determined to look cheerful no matter how bad Willie appeared in the light of day. Even so, the sight of his battered face nearly took her breath away. The cuts had darkened, and the black stitching thread showed up in jagged crisscrosses on forehead, chin, and cheekbone.

Jane crossed quickly to where he lay near the fire, a threadbare coverlet over his legs. The arm in a sling rested on his chest, but he reached out his good hand to her.

"Thank you for your help," he said through puffy lips.

"How is your arm?" Jane forced herself to look at him without wincing. "I am sure it's very painful."

"Doc says there's no infection yet."

Jane patted his shoulder. "That's excellent news."

"He won't be thatching any roofs though," Molly said. "Not for a long time."

Jane took a deep breath and stepped into the opening Molly had created. "Willie, you weren't helping your father thatch roofs when you got beaten on Johnson Road, were you?"

Molly's face filled with a combination of terror and anger. "Don't make Willie talk about that terrible night."

"Molly, I've learned recently that many villagers are involved in smuggling goods from Southampton's harbor." She searched Willie's face, but it was still as stone. "I couldn't imagine why your son and husband were out so late on a lonely stretch of road, but if they were smuggling contraband—"

"Get out of my house!" roared a voice behind Jane.

She whipped around, caught her foot, and nearly fell onto

the bed. Steadying herself, she faced the battered, beaten head of the home, Robert Lumb.

Molly jumped up. "Miss Austen came to see how our Willie was getting on. She helped the doctor set his arm, and she helped with your injuries as well."

"That gives her no right to make accusations."

Glad that her skirt hid her shaking knees, Jane stood her ground and stared at Robert Lumb's discolored face. "I've talked to several villagers. I know what's going on."

Mr. Lumb limped across the room, making an obviously painful effort to stand tall before lowering himself slowly into a chair by the fire. Although Jane found it stifling in the room for July, both the Lumb men seemed to find the heat comforting.

Jane took a chance and moved closer. She hoped that Mr. Lumb felt beholden enough to her that he wouldn't physically throw her out—if he could. "I was surprised to even find several churchgoing families involved in the town's smuggling scheme."

Robert snorted. "Don't churchgoin' folks need to eat same as the rest?"

"Of course. I only meant that they didn't see much wrong with such illegal—not to mention dangerous—activity."

"We all got to survive," he said, staring into the glowing embers.

"Then why weren't my sister and I asked to participate? We can sew dresses for illegal export that look as good as our neighbors' across the lane." She had figured out what the neighbor women were doing with all the clothes they sewed and that the man "stealing" from them was picking up bundles of clothing to transport south.

Robert Lumb twisted around then, his swollen lip curling in what was surely a painful sneer. "With your two brothers being officers in the navy, would we likely invite you to be part of it? You'd report us to them."

"Of course I would have. My brothers—and many of the villagers—have been fighting and dying for years on the open seas during this war with France. Yet you're trading with the French. Have you no shame for that?"

Willie groaned then, and Jane wished she had held her tongue. She'd almost forgotten he was lying right behind her.

Robert struggled to his feet and leaned over Jane, his eyes mere slits with anger. "You have no idea what it's like for the village."

"Of course I know," Jane protested. "I live here."

"You live in a free cottage. I don't see you lined up with the tenants to pay rent."

"Well, no, but we must live very frugally and prudently." She glanced down at her worn and mended skirt. "We don't dress differently than other women."

"Maybe not, but you Austen women travel around the country, visiting your rich relatives. We don't have money to travel or rich relatives. You keep two servants. Do you see any servants around here?" He swept an arm wide.

"We grow vegetables like the rest of the village and raise chickens," Jane protested.

"While you get an endless supply of milk from the squire's cows."

Jane dropped her gaze. She couldn't deny what he said. While they lived off their small legacies and Jane's even smaller writing income, she knew many villagers probably envied them. Daily they watched the Austens' manservant walk to Chawton House with Cassandra's dog, Link, who would carry home the pail of milk in his mouth. "That doesn't make smuggling any less illegal," Jane said quietly, retying her bonnet strings.

But as she left the Lumbs' dismal cottage, she wondered if she would feel so strongly if she walked in their shoes. Robert Lumb was wrong, yet his reasons made perfect sense.

12

Cabot Falls, Vermont
Present Day

Leaving the movie theater, Sofia felt compelled to drive by the accident site. The house at 618 Juniper Road was white with dark green trim. Although too early for blooming flowers, beds were cleaned and ready for planting when the last frost passed. An Easter banner flew by the kitchen door, and Easter bunny decals adorned the windows.

Sofia slowed the car as she passed and felt a chill when she noticed the rubber tire mark on the curb. How old was it? Could the police tell? She remembered the scraped mark on her own front tire that the officer had photographed.

She drove around the block to swing by for another look. Slowing to a crawl, she was embarrassed when a woman stepped out the door and pointedly stared at her car. "Oh crud," Sofia muttered. She'd been spotted. She couldn't very well speed off without looking guilty. Sighing, she pulled into the woman's driveway and got out.

"Hello," she called, reminding herself she had nothing to feel guilty about. As she walked up the sidewalk, she spotted a little boy on the other side of the glass storm door, pressing his nose against the window and then licking it. *If that was the toddler in the wagon, he looks happy and healthy*, Sofia thought with relief.

"Who are you?" the woman asked. Her expression wasn't hostile, but she was guarded. "Why are you back?"

Sofia was startled. "Back?"

"I saw you go by earlier. Now that you're parked, I see that it's the same kind of car that nearly hit my boy on Monday."

"There are lots of this make and model around."

"Not with that license plate number." She moved to block her son from sight as if she thought Sofia might hurt him.

"I wasn't driving my car that day," Sofia said.

"I know. It was a blonde."

Sofia's heart skipped a beat. "You saw the driver yourself?"

"Yes." She pushed back a wispy red curl that had escaped from her butterfly clip. "I was on the sidewalk, pulling my son in his wagon, when the car jumped the curb. It ran right over his trike and flattened it."

"It all must have happened so fast," Sofia said. "Could you really identify the driver?" She searched the young woman's face, waiting for her answer.

"I reported longish blond hair and a red coat or sweater." She shrugged. "I never said I could identify anyone."

"That's understandable. I'm sure you instinctively grabbed your son."

She zipped up her windbreaker. "I've never moved that fast in my life."

"Then how did you get the license plate number at the same time?" Sofia hated to call the woman a liar, but she'd admitted she didn't even see a face.

"I didn't give the police your license number," she said. "My neighbor next door did. She was talking with me while I traipsed up and down the sidewalk, enjoying a bit of sun." She nodded next door. "Do you want to ask her?"

"No, I don't think so. Thank you for talking to me." Sofia

started toward her car and then turned around. "I'm very glad your son wasn't hurt. I have four children of my own."

Sofia backed out of the driveway and headed home. She hadn't accomplished anything by talking to the woman, but the image of that funny little toddler kept coming back to her. She couldn't let people think that Vanessa had recklessly endangered—nearly killed—that little boy.

Unfortunately, Vanessa's innocence alone wouldn't get her out of trouble—if indeed she was innocent.

Chawton Village, England
July 1812

The night after visiting the Lumbs, Jane lay awake, envying Cassandra's gentle, even breathing. Her sister believed that their innocent ignorance would keep them out of trouble, but Jane knew differently.

What was she going to do? Should she report the smuggling if the villagers refused to stop? While Cassandra and Mamma had promised not to accept any more such "gifts" from neighbors, Jane had no faith that they'd be sheltered from the consequences if the smuggling was uncovered. Didn't her sister and mother ever read the London newspaper that Henry sent them? Accounts of smugglers imprisoned or hanged were frequent front-page reports.

Slipping from her bed, Jane pushed the window up several more inches, holding her breath when the casement squeaked. If only she could get a breath of moving air. She wrung a cloth out in cool water at the wash basin and then wiped her face and neck and arms. Back at the window, the air felt cooler on her damp skin.

The moon shone down benignly. Sound carried in the stillness, and their donkey across the small courtyard sounded restless in his stall.

Back in bed, Jane counted Cassandra's breaths, trying to match her sister's rhythm and eventually fall asleep. But Jane's mind slid from image to gory image—some real, some imagined—keeping her brain on high alert: bones poking through skin, beaten villagers, her own mother being led to the gallows . . .

She crawled out of bed one more time. Straightening her rumpled nightdress, Jane lifted her braid off her warm back. She smoothed her sheets again and lay down. She had nearly drifted off when the sounds of footsteps and muffled voices made her eyes snap open.

She waited, her heart thumping. *Was I dreaming?* No. There was the noise again, louder. She padded to the window and looked out on the moonlit courtyard below. Nothing moved, at least nothing her eye could see.

But the voices were louder. Muffled, but definitely louder, as if they were coming closer.

Her view was limited from their bedchamber window, so she threw on her dressing gown and hurried down the long upstairs hall to the high window at the end that overlooked the flower gardens. Peering down, she drew in her breath sharply.

Lanterns. Two of them. No, three lanterns were bobbing beneath the trees, now coming alongside their cottage past the kitchen vegetable garden. A group of four men stopped directly below her. One looked up to the second-story window, and Jane jerked back out of sight.

Who were they? What were they doing?

The group was huddled outside the cellar entrance. The double-door hatch was flat on the ground, secured by a heavy bar underneath, on the cellar side. Were they going to break in?

While the Austen women had no use for the cellar—they didn't own enough belongings to need it—Jane had been down there once. It was large, dug under two-thirds of the cottage.

Chawton Cottage had once served as an alehouse at the crossroads of the main highways. The double doors were opened wide then to allow barrels of ale to be rolled into the cellar.

Jane inched back to the window, standing to the side this time, and peered over the edge and down. No one was looking up now, but what were they doing down there?

Then her eyes adjusted, and she realized that one door of the hatch was open and lying flat on the grass outside. They'd broken in. But how could they have done it so quietly? Had the bar been removed so it was no longer locked?

Heart hammering, Jane raced back to the bedchamber and shook Cassandra's shoulder. "Wake up," Jane said. Cassandra's eyes blinked open and then closed again. "Wake up. Intruders!"

Cassandra's eyes flew open at that, but Jane swiftly covered her mouth. "Shhh. Come with me." She felt around for her own slippers and also found Cassandra's. She only hoped her whispers didn't carry out the bedchamber window and down to the courtyard below.

After lighting their tallow candle, Jane led the way. She could still hear Mamma's snoring, and Jane prayed fervently that she would sleep through whatever was about to happen.

Down the steep stairs and into the sitting room, Jane cupped her hand around the candle flame. If someone outside peered in the window, they'd realize the flickering candle meant someone was alert to the intrusion. She handed the candle to Cassandra, then pulled two long sticks of wood from the pile by the fireplace. She traded one for the candle and nodded for Cassandra to follow her to the kitchen.

Even before she reached the cellar stairs, Jane heard the voices below. She couldn't make out the words, but at least one of them sounded angry.

Jane leaned close to Cassandra, her lips tickled by her sister's hair, and whispered in her ear. "I saw four men outside. They're in the cellar now. You go and find the watchmen. They'll be patrolling the streets somewhere. If the men in the cellar try to come up these stairs, I'll knock them back down." She swung her wooden club to demonstrate.

Cassandra seemed frozen to the spot, so Jane gave her a slight shove, which broke her trance. Cassandra then raced out of the room, her long braid bouncing on her back, and Jane soon heard the click of the front door.

Ear pressed to the cellar door, Jane tried to make out words, but she couldn't. Feet shuffled, and she heard wooden crates being moved. *What was that?* She knew for a fact that the cellar was empty. At least, it had been the last time she was down there.

She jumped at the sounds of a crash and glass breaking, followed by cursing like Jane had never heard. The words might be new, but she had definitely heard that voice before. Robert Lumb. *How dare he break in!*

Jane jerked open the cellar door. She thrust her flickering candle in front of her, but the candle only made a small circle of light a few steps down.

Voices and movement below halted abruptly.

Foul, musty air rose up to meet Jane as she slowly descended the rough stairs, her candle held in front of her. Dank coldness brushed her face despite the warmth of the hot July night. At the bottom of the stairs, Jane's flickering candle threw monstrous shadows on boxes and barrels and stone walls . . . and four men poised to spring at her. A reeking stench of whiskey filled the cellar, which explained the sound of breaking glass.

Jane barely noticed the smell as she faced the deadly stare of Robert Lumb. "And to what, may I ask, do I owe this call in the middle of the night?"

No one said a word in reply. Jane stepped forward, lifting the candle in the faces of the men. Two of them she recognized from church, and they looked sheepish. But Mr. Lumb and the scrawny man behind him with an eye patch looked ready to pounce.

"What's in the boxes and crates under the tarps?" Jane demanded. "And how did you get in?" She walked across the gritty floor, through dust and swaying cobwebs, to the double doors set into the cellar's ceiling. The wooden bar, which should have kept the double doors locked, was leaning against the wall. "I expect that you conveniently left the bar off the doors after storing your merchandise here." She swung around, nearly extinguishing her candle and making shadows jump in wild confusion. "But how did you get in here in the first place? You have no right to be here."

And where is Cassandra with some help? she wondered, wishing now that she'd waited in the kitchen.

"Nobody was using this cellar," Robert grumbled. "So we put it to good use."

"You mean you needed a place to hide your smuggled goods, with innocent people where the law wouldn't think to look." Jane was infuriated. "I'm reporting you to the constable."

Unexpectedly, Robert Lumb broke out in loud guffaws. "Better yet, get your brother the squire down here." He leaned in close, his cuts and bruises giving him an evil look. "We'll explain to him how his mother gave us permission to use her cellar."

Jane's mouth dropped open. "Mamma?" She squinted. "You're lying."

Robert's one-eyed shadow swaggered over to stand behind Jane, and she winced at the combined smells of sweat and whiskey.

"We came by one day when you young ladies were out," Lumb said. "Mrs. Austen gave us permission to store things here. Ask her. She took the bar off the double doors herself and told us to use that entrance."

"She never told us anything about this," Jane said, "and I seriously doubt that you told her you'd be storing contraband here."

Robert bowed low. "She was eager to help in exchange for some brandy and the occasional ham."

Jane fumed, breathing hard. Mamma would never make a deal like that. But, she admitted to herself, Mamma could have been tricked, persuaded that Mr. Lumb simply didn't have enough storage space in their tiny rented cottage.

"Regardless of what Mamma told you, get this out of our cellar now."

"We won't be moving anything yet." Robert shrugged. "Sorry about the smell of the whiskey. Clumsy oaf dropped the case." He motioned for the other men to take two tarp-covered crates and leave. "When it's time to deliver the other stuff, we'll be back."

"If any of this contraband is still here in the morning, I'm getting the constable." Jane looked over her shoulder and up the cellar stairs where Cassandra peered down anxiously. At the sound of feet on the outside cellar stairs, Jane whipped around. Two men were clomping in heavy boots down into the cellar—two of the town's watchmen, the Jacobson brothers from down the street.

Thank you, Lord, Jane prayed. "And now I have two witnesses."

At that, Robert Lumb burst out laughing. Disconcerted, Jane glanced up at Cassandra, who shook her head in bewilderment. Robert slung one arm over each twin's shoulders. "Miss Austen, meet the two best haulers in our little enterprise."

Jane stiffened but got hold of herself and stood her ground. "I don't care if you've involved the whole town. Get this out of here by morning, or I turn you all in. And if the constable is a smuggler too, my brother will find one who isn't."

Whatever it took, her family couldn't hide smuggled goods in their cellar. It was so dangerous. How long had it been there? Months?

"Think about your families." Jane turned to the two silent ones standing with shoulders hunched. "What will happen to them if you hang or go to prison?" They shuffled their feet on the sandy floor. "Robert, your own son was nearly killed and may still lose his arm. It's too dangerous, what you're doing."

"It's better than watching our wives and children starve."

"You heard what I said," Jane repeated, fighting to keep a tremor out of her voice. "You have until morning." She climbed the stairs to the kitchen, closed the door, and shoved sticks of wood beneath the door to jam it closed. She fell into Cassandra's arms, and they stumbled to the sitting room, shivering despite the July heat. They rocked for nearly an hour before Cassandra said she might be able to sleep again.

Jane carried the candle to her writing desk.

The whole smuggling scheme was too big for her to handle. She needed advice from her brothers. Before moving into Chawton Cottage three years ago, Jane had jokingly asked her brother Edward, "Does the history of this alehouse include smuggling?"

He had promptly teased her back. "Every alehouse in the country must. Brandy comes by stealth from France."

Only tonight's smuggled ale in the cellar was no joke. Lumb's dry-land smugglers were using their cellar as temporary storage as they moved contraband and sold it. Her mother and sister had received stolen goods, and she herself had eaten the food. How could she prove they were innocent?

The answer was simple. She couldn't. If they were caught, they'd be punished.

And what about her brothers? Charles and Frank risked their lives every day—and the lives of their crew—fighting in a war that included catching pirates and smugglers. If their own family was convicted as part of a smuggling ring, would they lose their careers in the navy?

With a heavy heart, Jane penned three letters. One was addressed to Francis Austen. Frank was captain of the *Elephant* somewhere in the Atlantic, engaged in the war with America. If only she could see a recent copy of the *Naval Chronicle*. It detailed Royal Navy actions, with maps and illustrations, and might have shown if her brothers' ships had changed ports.

Her second note was addressed to Captain Charles Austen on the ship *Namur*; he lived with his wife, Fanny, and their daughters aboard the ship. He was on harbor duty in the Thames estuary at the Nore, where the River Thames met the North Sea.

She had no idea how long it would take her letters to reach them or if indeed they would get there at all. They had a right to know what was going on, how their family's involvement could cast an evil shadow on them. While it might not mean a court-martial, to say it would be embarrassing was too light. More like a betrayal.

Jane dipped her pen in the ink and began. Without naming names, she described recent events in the village and how the Austen women had become involved. She ended both letters with the same plea: "How can I stop what's going on before it's too late?"

Her third short note was to brother Henry at his bank in London, asking that he visit Chawton as soon as possible.

The one brother she didn't tell—and wouldn't until she had no choice—was Edward, the Squire of Chawton Village. As squire, he would be duty-bound to prosecute every smuggler, including his own mother and sisters. Jane had hopes, slim as they were, that she could somehow halt the smuggling ring before the squire needed to hear of it. While he undoubtedly knew that such activity occurred in coastal towns, he probably had no idea that the villagers in Chawton had their own private smuggling ring.

Or that contraband was being stored in his own Chawton Cottage.

13

Cabot Falls, Vermont
Present Day

After leaving the house at 618 Juniper Road, Sofia passed by downtown stores. Julie's text message floated to the top of a brain filled with jumbled thoughts: "Are you ready to sign the lease?" She still wasn't ready to call Julie. But, she thought, swinging her car in the direction of the library, she could talk to Marla about it. Even though Marla obviously loved the idea of a shop on the square too, talking to her wouldn't be like encountering the steamroller that was Julie.

Sofia loved everything about the Victorian building that housed their public library: the marble-floored main lobby, carved woodwork, ornate tin ceiling, and stained glass windows. She peeked into the reading and reference rooms but didn't spot Marla. Then, around the corner, Marla waved from behind her horseshoe desk where she was helping a patron use the new computer checkout system.

After she was free, Marla pushed her reading glasses up on her head. "Come back to my office for some coffee if you have time."

"I do if you do," Sofia said, following her friend to her office. "I know you're working, but I wanted to ask you something."

"Sure. Shoot." Marla poured coffee into two mugs, one that read, "A library is cool—check it out!" and the other with a famous quote by Louisa May Alcott: "She is too fond of books, and it has addled her brain."

Sofia took a sip, then blew on the scalding liquid. "After thinking about it, how do you feel about leasing the shop on the square? Can you commit to running a business during evenings and weekends after working here full time?"

"That's the million-dollar question. I've wrestled with it, and I've talked it over with Tim." Tim was her fifteen-year-old son. "Being both father and mother to him takes time, and I won't forfeit that. He'll be gone in a few short years."

"I feel exactly the same way."

"Tim thinks I should go for it though. Maybe cut back to part time here, if the board will let me, and eventually retire."

"Do you have money to lose if the shop isn't a success right away?" Sofia pulled on her purse strap, twisting it around her finger. "We don't unless I dip into the kids' college funds, and I won't do that."

"No, of course not. You have to do what's right for you and your family."

"But I think Julie has her heart set on this."

Marla grinned. "Don't tell me. You're getting hourly calls and texts too?"

"Not quite, but almost." Sofia clicked Marla's coffee mug with her own. "I'll decide soon. I promise."

Marla drained her coffee mug and set it aside. "Now, how's that third quilt square coming along? You know how I love research." She nodded at the poster on her wall: "Archives—born to be filed."

Sofia hesitated, suddenly needing to confide in someone. "Every time I get started on the quilt square, I find police at the door."

"What?"

Briefly, she told Marla what had happened that week with Vanessa and what she feared might still happen. Marla was as supportive as Sofia had known she would be.

Sofia rubbed her forehead. "I love my kids to pieces, but there are weeks I'd like to retire too—from motherhood."

Chawton Village, England
July 1812

Although Jane retired to her bed hours after Cassandra, she was first to awaken when sunlight struck her full in the face. The drapes still gaped open from when she'd peered out in the night to the courtyard below. It was a measure of their distress that neither she nor Cassandra had noticed or pulled the drapes closed after the excitement was over.

She dressed hurriedly, taking care to avoid the creaky boards beneath the rugs in the bedchamber. She'd wash later. She was eager to check the cellar before Mamma woke up, hoping against hope that the smugglers had heeded her warning to remove the contraband and she wouldn't have to report anyone yet. Holding her shoes in hand, Jane crept down the narrow stairs to the ground floor. Good. Not even the servants were anywhere in evidence.

In the kitchen, she yanked the sticks of wood away from beneath the cellar door. She lit a lantern hanging on a hook and started downstairs.

In the night she'd been able to see so little by the light of her tallow candle, but the lantern illuminated much better. Dusty crates and casks were still covered with mildewed tarps. Small bales of tobacco and tea sat in one corner. Obviously the men didn't take her threat seriously. She pressed a handkerchief to her nose. The smell of whiskey was nearly overpowering.

Her jaw clenched when she remembered the previous night, how she'd been so relieved when Cassandra had arrived with the town watchmen to save them. She'd laugh if it didn't make her so angry. The very men entrusted by the people of Chawton with their safety were crooked. But what could she do? What could one spinster lady do against a town full of smugglers?

She turned slowly, her lantern throwing bobbing shadows on the whitewashed walls. Partly to see better and mostly to dissipate the smell of spirits, Jane made her way up the four short steps to the outside double doors. They were still unlocked but much heavier than she'd guessed. Her push on one door allowed in two inches of sunlight before it crashed back down. After two more tries, she gave up.

Holding her lantern high, she rummaged in several crates and wooden boxes. She emptied two boxes and then filled them with an assortment of the smugglers' treasure to show the constable. Some of it, like the brandy, had clearly been smuggled in for resale to others. Several boxes held wrapped bundles of finished dresses, jackets, and shawls for smuggling out of England and into France for sale.

The only thing that tempted Jane was the tea. They'd been doing without while all the time, there was a bale of it in their cellar.

Jane ascended the cellar steps at the same time their maid and manservant appeared in the kitchen.

"Oh, Miss Jane, you give me a start," Eliza said.

"I'm sorry. I was tending to some business," she said.

Thomas, a loyal and caring middle-aged grandfather, took the lantern from her. "Can I help you, miss?" His eyes clearly asked what in the world she was doing in the cellar.

"Yes, you can, Thomas," Jane said. "Two boxes at the foot of the stairs are to be carried outside and put in the donkey cart, one on the seat and one on the floorboard. Use one of the tarps from the cellar to cover the boxes. Harness the donkey then." Jane sighed. How she missed having horses, but only families like the Rutledges seemed to own horses these days. "Meet me in the cellar after you open the outside doors."

"Yes, miss. Shall I get the wood in first?"

"No, boxes first. I want to be on my way to Alton."

Eliza bustled around, stirring the fire, filling the kettle, and slicing bread for their breakfast. "You best eat before you go."

"Fix some bread and cheese to take along," Jane said. She intended to be on the road to Alton early with the farm laborers. She wanted news of her departure to be spread fast by the Chawton gossips. Those involved needed to know she was serious about reporting them.

Jane went back down to the cellar when she heard Thomas thrust one cellar door wide open, then the other. Light and clean air poured in the open hatch from the fresh July morning.

While Thomas was clearly surprised at the contents of the cellar, he said nothing. Jane pointed to the boxes, and he carried them out. By the time Jane got her bonnet, shawl, and bread, he'd loaded the wooden boxes and covered them with a tarp.

Jane was glad to get away before Cassandra or Mamma awakened and tried to stop her. Thomas gave Jane a hand up into the donkey cart. At the same time, Eliza called out the back door, "I need that wood."

Thomas handed Jane the reins, nodded, and headed inside.

Jane flicked the reins. The donkey twitched his long ears and reluctantly moved forward. "I know it's early," Jane said, "but it's still cool. Pick up your feet." While her voice sounded confident, her insides were quaking. Villagers would see her the moment she entered the lane and would report her to Lumb or the watchmen.

The donkey moved across the courtyard behind the cottage and began to turn by the corner of the house. Without warning, a man jumped out and grabbed the donkey's harness. The donkey shook his head, jerking back and forth, but the burly man held tight.

Robert Lumb. His angry scowl looked even more evil than it had in the night.

"Where do you think you're going?" He darted to the side of the cart and, in one swift move, yanked the tarp aside. "Who's smuggling now?"

"Let go of the harness. I'm going to Alton to see the constable."

"And report your own mother?" He laughed harshly. "You'd never pay a toll to see the constable." He referred to the payment exacted from anyone driving a conveyance on the main roads. Those who walked were never charged a toll.

"I'm taking evidence with me, Mr. Lumb. And while I am stronger than the average fainting female, even I cannot carry two crates in my arms."

His smile disappeared. He jumped up to balance on the floorboard, bringing his bruised, discolored face close to hers. Jane flicked the reins. The donkey jolted ahead and knocked Robert Lumb to the ground. Jane braced her feet against the floorboard as she rounded the corner of the cottage.

He bounded up and in two swift strides, he grabbed the donkey's harness again.

And then, to Jane's complete and utter shock, Cassandra ran up from behind them. Barefoot and in her nightdress, she held a pitchfork out in front of her and raced straight at Robert Lumb.

He yelled, let go of the harness, jumped back, and fell to the ground. Jane pulled hard on the reins to stop the braying donkey from dancing and kicking Mr. Lumb.

"Are you unharmed, Jane?" Cassandra called, her eyes and sharp pitchfork tines focused on the fallen man.

"Yes, I'm safe." Jane glanced over her shoulder. "Where did you come from?"

"I saw you from the bedchamber window." Panting, she tossed her waist-length graying hair over her back. "I sneaked down through the cellar and out into the courtyard to get the fork from the granary."

Robert Lumb held a hand before his face and began sliding backward in the gravel.

"It's all right, Cassandra. Let him up."

Robert Lumb stood, warily eyeing the pitchfork, and raised both hands in the air. "Let's talk before you go to the constable."

Jane resolved not to let the relief show on her face. He couldn't know that she'd hoped desperately for that very thing.

Jane took the pitchfork and threw Cassandra her shawl. "I gave you time last night to clear out our cellar. Nothing has been moved."

"I'll move it right now. I'll get a wagon, and your manservant can help me load it."

"You will not involve Thomas. No."

"Don't push me."

Jane gripped the pitchfork. "Don't tempt me."

Swallowing his fury, he relented. "I'll have it moved in an hour."

Jane pretended to consider it, waiting until the confident arrogance drained from the man's face. Finally, she nodded. "Unless it's gone in one hour, there's no deal."

"Yes ma'am." His words were polite, but his tone dripped venom.

After Robert Lumb left, Jane turned to Cassandra. "After you dress, might we walk in the direction of Alton together? I should like to unburden myself of something." *And mail my letters privately*, she thought. She had no doubt that the smuggled goods would be gone when they returned.

Jane circled the kitchen garden and waited for Cassandra near the shrubbery. She collapsed on a bench, suddenly exhausted. Nearby, the chickens clucked and scratched in the dirt. The July heat heightened the scents in their cottage garden, which was filled with those flowers that could fend for themselves. Usually the sweet aroma of the hollyhocks, delphiniums, lilies, and roses stilled Jane's distressed heart. But the events during the dark of night and again this morning had left her numb to nature's delights. A walk to Alton and a talk with dear Cassandra were exactly what she needed.

"I've written to Frank and Charles," Jane said as soon as they set off for their daily exercise to talk without Mamma's interruptions. "I'm posting them in Alton though."

"A wise plan," Cassandra agreed. "One doesn't know anymore who is a smuggler and who isn't. Things are not at all as they seem."

"With the cool reception I received at the shop last week, I worry that my letters could accidentally get 'lost.'"

"Oh, Jane, what should we do? Our friends are involved. They aren't professional smugglers or pirates. They'll be discovered."

"Yes, and go to prison or be hung," Jane agreed. "I do not understand how they can take such chances. It means leaving their families to starve with no means of support."

Jane swung along the lane toward Alton, a town as familiar to her as her home. Strolling by Hampshire farms and the low, wooded hills usually filled her with peace. The rushing of a stream, the warm smell of turned earth, the call of a curlew wading in a puddle . . .

But her thoughts were in turmoil this morning, and she was no nearer a solution when they reached the milestone marking the distances to London—forty-eight miles—and Winchester—sixteen miles. Up ahead were the railway bridges at the Alton end of Winchester Road. Although her mind whirled around and around for several miles, she was as undecided about what to do as when Cassandra had rushed at Robert Lumb with a pitchfork.

She laughed aloud at the memory.

"Jane, what is it?"

"Remembering you in your nightdress, hair streaming behind you, as you charged at Robert Lumb with the pitchfork."

"I cannot believe I did that," Cassandra said. "Thank you for your shawl."

They passed the tollhouse, but since they were on foot, there was no toll to be paid. The display board listed charges for various types of carriages. While some villagers lamented the increase in traffic on the well-maintained toll roads, Jane was grateful. With the increase in traffic, there had been a marked decrease in highwaymen. With more people on the roads, it was more difficult for robbers to carry out their crimes and escape.

It must be harder for smugglers too, Jane realized. They probably had to stick to back roads and the woods. That would explain why Willie and Robert Lumb were attacked on such a remote road.

After Jane left her letters at the Alton posting station, she and Cassandra strolled past a dozen houses and shops. They bought scones to eat on the walk home and a freshly plucked chicken from the poulterer for the evening meal.

On the way back out of town, Jane spotted the mail coach coming through. Her letters should be on their way without delay. Mail coaches changed teams in less than five minutes at some posting stations, but today they didn't even stop. The mail carrier dropped a bag as they trotted by the Alton posting station, and a man tossed a bag of letters up to him. Since mail coaches were not required to stop and pay a toll, it sped on past the gate.

"They must be going ten miles per hour," Jane said, covering her mouth and nose against the dust the coach stirred up.

Back home, Jane delivered the chicken to Eliza and then took a candle and descended into the cellar. It had been cleaned out. Heavy drag marks crisscrossed the sandy floor, but that was the only sign that remained of the smuggling. The double cellar doors were barred with two stout pieces of wood.

Cassandra stood on the cellar steps. "Thankfully, it's over."

Jane shook her head. "It's not over, not at all. I'll go back to writing by the window. Only now I'll pay attention to events happening right under my nose. They'll need to take a trip to Southampton soon."

Cassandra frowned. "Why?"

"It's the nearest port, and they have garments to sell to smugglers who will transport the goods to France." Southampton was only about three hours away. "When they make their move, I plan to be ready."

She was still missing a big piece of the puzzle though, and she knew she'd only discover it by secretly following the villagers to Southampton. Someone on the other end had to be their go-between. But who? How were they connecting with smugglers from France? Surely no one from Chawton knew such a person.

Cassandra interrupted her thoughts. "I'm worried about you, Jane. Must you continue, now that we're out of it?"

"I can't stop now. If their luck runs out, half of Chawton could be implicated. If that happens, they will accuse us, whether the cellar is empty or not."

Jane felt Robert Lumb's hostile glare all over again, and she shivered. No, if the Lumbs were caught, he would make sure the whole Austen family went down with the ship.

14

Cabot Falls, Vermont
Present Day

"Vanessa was caught skipping school too," Sofia confided to Marla as they sat in her library office. "I don't know how it's all going to turn out, but thanks so much for listening. It really helped."

"Parenting isn't for the faint of heart. We're all in this together." Marla glanced at the clock. "Would you like to tell me about your third quilt square? Do you have time?"

Sofia smiled, glad for a change of topic. For the next few minutes, she laid out what she'd found, what the translation hinted at, and what websites she'd checked out. "So, it seems at least a possibility that Jane Austen embroidered the square, if I ever discover the missing link of how the square came into the possession of my Italian ancestors."

Marla tilted her head, squinting. "Hmmm. You said 'stowaway' was mentioned in the diary?"

"I'm almost positive that's the correct translation."

"After hours, I'll see what I can find on my genealogy sites. I had such fun helping with the first two quilt blocks." She refreshed their coffee. "It could take awhile, but I'll see what I can find."

"Thanks, Marla, I really appreciate that."

"It makes me feel like Sherlock Holmes," she said grinning. "Now, let's see what else we can find about Jane's embroidery. She wasn't a rich woman. I'd be surprised if she dressed in much silk."

Sofia watched as Marla's fingers flew over the keyboard, getting into national archives, university libraries, and government sites that only her library connection would give her access to. "Look here," she said. "It's the right time frame, and it might explain why Jane Austen would quilt a square in silk."

Sofia leaned closer to the computer and read aloud. "Silk ribbon embroidery was also popular. During this period, a great deal of a woman's time was spent visiting and being visited. While one ought not to pull out the mending to repair in front of company, it was perfectly acceptable to take along some piece of fancy needlework to stitch on while chatting. Cushion covers were embroidered and handkerchiefs monogrammed, giving the worker a chance to show off one of her accomplishments and allowing her companions to marvel at the tiny size and accuracy of her stitches."

"That sounds promising," Marla said. "A lady's handkerchief would be white and about the size of your quilt square."

"But would a handkerchief be trimmed in lace?"

"Not for everyday use, surely," Marla said, "but for something fancy, like a wedding."

Something clicked with Sofia from all her reading. "Jane's sister, Cassandra, was engaged. Maybe she made it for her. Her fiancé died, and she never married. Jane might have been making it as a surprise, but kept it after the fiancé died. Or maybe she made it for a niece. She had lots of nieces."

"But if it was for a sister or niece, I think it would say 'love' instead of 'in friendship,' don't you?" Marla motioned for Sofia to pull her chair closer. "Did you notice this site? Jane Austen's House Museum."

"I was reading on it last night."

"It says they have some original letters and sometimes parts of manuscripts on display. Don't you wish you could see them in person?"

Sofia clicked on several links to letters, looking for any Italian connection. After the third, she laughed out loud. "Read that. I love it."

The short letter, framed on the museum wall, was a note from a man to Jane. He sounded like her agent or publisher or maybe a fan. He was trying to persuade Jane to write gothic romances, as it was proven that they sold much better than her stories of "simple village life."

"A lot he knew," Marla said. "Her response is a stitch."

Sofia read it again. Jane had told the man that she loved writing about a few families in a village, and if she had to write gothic romances, she'd rather hang herself. "Can you email me the link to this page?" Sofia asked. "I may print it out and frame it."

How Sofia admired Jane, both as a writer and a woman. Jane had gone against the odds and followed her dream in the early 1800s when very few women were publishing. Jane didn't "sell out" either. The man's well-meant suggestion to write gothic romances wasn't her. She knew she'd be miserable, trying to fit her square peg into a round hole.

Sofia understood her feeling exactly. It was precisely how she felt about Julie's idea of drawing caricatures on the sidewalk and teaching cartoon art classes. She wouldn't hang herself, but it sounded like its own brand of misery.

After finally speaking her worries aloud with Marla, Sofia felt a tidal wave of exhaustion wash over her as she drove home. Forget caricatures. Forget Jane Austen. Forget her catering business. All she cared about was where the investigation stood. Why had they heard nothing more from the police?

Chawton Village, England
July 1812

A week after mailing her letters, Jane had heard nothing from either naval brother. She hadn't expected to hear from Frank yet, with him waging war on the high seas. But with Charles's ship anchored in the Thames, he should have received her shocking letter and sent a reply by now. It only took a day or two for the mail to travel from London to Chawton.

A disturbing thought occurred to her: Would someone at the postal station accidentally "lose" any mail coming from her brothers? She should have told her brothers to mail replies to nearby Alton.

While recopying more chapters of *Pride and Prejudice*, Jane had spent hours at the window again, looking out on the Winchester and London-to-Gosport Roads. So far she'd spotted either Robert Lumb or Mr. Powell pass by every day, and Cassandra had seen them in the shop. While they might have made short trips to neighboring villages during the week to sell off the contraband brandy and tobacco, they hadn't been gone long enough to pick up another smuggled shipment in Southampton. Judging from the bundles of finished garments that had been removed from the cellar, Jane knew the time to deliver the garments to the smugglers must be soon.

And she would be ready.

All she needed was some inside information first. Jane felt certain she could coax it from Anne Powell, given the chance, but Jane knew she'd not be welcome in the Powell house after her confrontation with Mr. Powell. Still, Anne had always been a dear friend.

Almost as if her thoughts had conjured up Anne's presence, she spotted her strolling, basket over her arm, down the road to Alton. As Jane raced to the front door and flung it open, she thanked heaven that Anne was alone.

"Anne," Jane called.

The girl stopped, nearly stumbled, then stared straight ahead and continued down the road.

"Anne, please. I must talk to you."

Anne glanced over her shoulder but kept on going down the road, her back straight and stiff.

"Anne, I'm still your friend," Jane called, saddened at the rebuff.

Anne did not appear to hear. However, as Jane watched in silence, Anne gave a slight jerk of her head. At the crossroads, she glanced over her shoulder again, then smoothly angled right and disappeared out of sight.

She's coming to the back door, Jane realized. She raced from the hall through the empty sitting room and kitchen. Anne was already waiting on the stoop when she opened the door.

Jane pulled the girl inside.

Anne flinched at her touch, but her expression held more confusion than disdain. Jane could only imagine what she'd heard from her father. "We must talk about the smuggling," Jane said, holding her arm to prevent flight.

Anne glanced into the sitting room and beyond to the hallway.

"It's all right. No one will overhear. Eliza walked to the Alton shops. Thomas is out back, blacking shoes and boots." Jane glanced up. "Cassandra is upstairs with Mamma, who is unwell. Cassandra reads to her and bathes her temples with vinegar water." She motioned for Anne to follow her.

But Anne remained rooted to the spot. "What do you want from me?"

Jane winced at the cold, unfriendly tone. "I want you to hear me out, and then I want you to help me and help your own family." She poured a cup of very weak tea from the pot and then motioned for Anne to follow her into the sitting room.

Jane waited for Anne to finally set her basket down and take a chair. Jane hardly knew where to start. She was certain that Robert Lumb was in charge of the village smugglers, but when was the next smuggling run to Southampton planned? And how had he made contact with a French smuggler who wanted British goods? From what her brothers had said, the small smuggling ships stayed out in the narrow strait where they could escape quickly. So, someone in the village must hire a boat to row out to meet the smugglers. But who?

If Jane was careful, she might coax the answer out of Anne. Even if her young friend truly believed she knew nothing about it, she had undoubtedly overheard things and knew more than she thought.

Anne sat with chin jutted out. "I'm not supposed to talk to you."

"I think you know that I only want to help. Few others talk to me either, but did you hear that I found smuggled goods down in our own cellar?"

"What?" Anne's hand jerked, making her tea slosh into the saucer.

Jane told her what had transpired a week earlier and finished with Cassandra going after Robert Lumb with a pitchfork.

"I had no idea," Anne said, her voice a hoarse whisper.

"I'm now sure Robert Lumb is in charge of the smuggling ring in Chawton. I believe that's why he and his son were so badly beaten a couple of weeks ago."

"I don't understand."

"I expect they were traveling to or from another village to sell the contraband and ran into highwaymen. They stole either their goods or the money they'd collected, then beat them as some kind of warning not to return. This is dangerous business, Anne. And it needs to be stopped."

"But my father would never be involved in such things."

"He admitted to me that he was," Jane said. "That's why you were forbidden to talk to me."

Jane watched disbelief and fear grow in Anne's eyes. She pulled her chair closer. "I hope you will tell me anything you've overheard at home, something that might indicate when they plan to travel to Southampton next."

"I haven't heard anything."

"Anne, you must help me convince them to stop the smuggling. It's so dangerous."

"Jane, I believe that you care about me and my family," Anne said, setting her tea down and grabbing her basket, "but you must be imagining things."

Jane clenched her fists. Did no one else read the London papers? How could Anne willfully ignore the dangers involved?

"What I'm telling you is true. You didn't see Robert and Willie Lumb when they were brought back beaten and bleeding, with bones sticking through skin." Anne winced, but Jane went on. "Imagine your own father and brother in that state. And that's trifling compared to what would happen to them if they were caught. They'd be tried for treason. Your mother too, if she knows what's happening. Smugglers who are caught—men and women both—are tried as traitors."

Anne swallowed hard. "What happens if they are found guilty?" she barely whispered.

"Some are hung. Some are imprisoned. With overcrowded prisons, many are deported to the colonies."

"Deported?"

"Many are sent to Australia where they are assigned to work gangs for years."

Anne looked like she was close to fainting, but Jane could see she still wasn't convinced enough to divulge anything she had heard.

Anne stood, her lips pressed together. "Papa says the war is nearly over. If he or my brother were imprisoned, it would be for a short time."

"Oh, don't be a simpleton!" Jane cried. "Even if they were lucky enough to go to a prison, they'd likely never come out."

"You're trying to scare me," Anne said, moving to the door.

"Of course I am—scare you with the truth. I can show you newspaper reports to prove everything I've said." Jane blocked her way. "Prisons are often tiny, run by individuals paid almost nothing. A third of the prisoners are now women. They are housed in filthy, rat-infested hovels with only dirty straw to sleep on. Food must be supplied by the prisoners' families or they don't eat. But prisons are overflowing. Your family would most likely be hung or deported."

Anne's face turned so pale that Jane helped her back to her chair before she fainted. Anne gulped several times. "I truly know of no plans to go to the coast."

"They might not talk about Southampton at all, but have you heard your father or brother talking about trips somewhere else?"

Anne thought for a moment but shook her head. "I can't think of any traveling plans they've mentioned."

Jane paced back and forth across the sitting room, desperately disappointed. She had pinned her hopes on Anne, but she believed now that she knew nothing.

"Except—" Anne ventured.

Jane whipped around eagerly. "Except what?"

"Papa told Mamma that he and my brother would be gone tomorrow, helping a farmer near Four Marks rebuild a barn destroyed by fire."

Jane tensed, then swiftly sat down again beside Anne. The village of Four Marks was only three miles south of Chawton, on Winchester Road heading to Southampton and on the edge of Chawton Park Wood. The story about the barn sounded plausible, except that wood was hard to find after their forests had been ravaged to build all the navy's ships. It was difficult to believe that anyone could rebuild a barn now. Jane's heart beat wildly. "Do you know if anyone else in Chawton is helping him rebuild?"

Anne hesitated, then nodded. "It was Mr. Lumb who asked Papa. Several are leaving before sunup tomorrow. Papa said they would stay the night there, maybe two nights, until they finish the barn."

Jane nodded, triumphant. That barn story was fiction as much as anything she'd written. The men might go through Four Marks, but their real destination was Southampton, where they'd meet up with smugglers from France. She'd bet her life on it.

Jane spent the next half hour convincing Anne to go with her and follow the men. "We'll drive our donkey cart. If they stop at Four Marks, then I'll gladly admit that I'm wrong. We'll enjoy our picnic food and come back home. But if I'm right"—she grasped Anne's slender hands in her own ink-stained ones—"we'll follow at a safe distance, well out of sight, all the way to Southampton. It should only take a day, even going slowly."

"And if it comes to that, after you find what you are looking for in Southampton, will you turn around and drive back during the night?"

"Heavens no." *What a naïve question*, Jane thought. Two women on the road alone at night? "Frank's wife, Mary, still lives in Southampton in Rose Cottage. We lived with her for three years while Frank was at sea before we moved to this blessed country village. We'll go to Mary's house." Jane thought for a moment. "Leave a note for your mother and tell her about Mary. It will ease her fears when she reads your note. Of course, you cannot tell anyone ahead of time. Your father and brother would stop you."

Anne nodded slowly, fear evident in her face, but determination was there too. "I'd better hurry and do the shopping or Mamma will wonder what took so long." She gathered her bonnet, basket, and reticule and then squared her thin shoulders. "After the men leave tomorrow and Mamma retires again to her bedchamber, I'll slip out. Shall I meet you in your back courtyard?"

"Yes, good," Jane agreed. "And take heart. If we stop them, we may be saving the families of half the village, including our own. But it must be done now. We can't wait any longer."

15

Cabot Falls, Vermont
Present Day

After leaving Marla and the library, Sofia decided she could wait no longer to talk to Vanessa. If she'd been able to find out that Vanessa was at the theater Monday afternoon—four blocks from the hit-and-run address—the police couldn't be far behind.

Sofia was ready for an argument, and it surprised her when Vanessa admitted to being at the movies.

"Who was with you?"

"Mo-om!"

"Why won't you name the person who could give you an alibi?"

"What good would it do now?" Vanessa asked. "That policeman won't believe anything we say. He'll claim that we had days to cook up an alibi. Even if I gave him the entire plot of the movie, he'd say I've had time to go back and see it now."

"But you have *proof*." Sofia waved the ticket stub. "Time- and date-stamped."

"That only proves I bought the ticket."

"Vanessa, you're not helping."

"I'm saying what that officer will say to me."

"Let's stop this. I remembered the call from Abby on Sunday and how you said it was 'all set' or something. I'm sure Abby went with you, or I will be, after your dad checks attendance records today." Sofia took a deep breath. "Are you hiding Abby's name from the police because *she* was driving my car?"

"No! I'd never give your keys to someone else."

Sofia studied her older daughter's slender frame. "I have to ask you something else then," she finally said.

Vanessa tilted her head to one side.

"Did you stay in the movie the whole time?"

"What do you mean? I wasn't going to spend the money and not watch it."

Sofia chose her words carefully. "I mean, did you leave the theater at all?"

Vanessa thought back. "I went to the restroom once." Then her eyes opened wide. "I see what you're asking." Hurt and disbelief were written on her face. "You want to know if I snuck out during the movie and tried to run over some little kid."

"Don't be like that. You know the police will ask since the house is only four blocks from the movie theater. I want to know what you'll say."

"I'll say I watched the whole movie. I can tell them what it was about and how it ended, even if they don't believe me. I didn't leave in the middle."

Sofia paced back and forth across the girls' room. "What about this? Did anything unusual happen during the show that would prove you were there? A baby screaming so the usher had to ask its mother to leave? The movie stopping partway through? Someone getting sick?"

Vanessa thought for a moment and then shook her head. "Sorry." She chewed her lower lip. "But something else did happen that I was afraid to tell you."

Sofia sat down on Vanessa's bed. "What?"

"I left the keys in the car again that afternoon. I didn't leave it running this time, thankfully."

"Oh, Vanessa."

"I know. I was laughing and talking to Abby, and I got distracted. I didn't notice until after the movie. At least I was sure I locked the car, and it was still there when I came out, in the same place."

"You got in by using the key in the magnetic holder?"

Vanessa nodded. "All's well that ends well, right?"

Sofia rubbed the back of her neck. This was far from the end. "If the keys were locked in the car all that time and my car hadn't moved, then my Suburban couldn't have been the one that jumped that curb during the movie."

"That's what I've been telling you all along."

"And yet, the description and license number described my car." *And the blond driver in red sounded like you*, Sofia added silently.

By Vanessa's expression, she had read her mother's thoughts.

Chawton Village, England
July 1812

Before sunrise the next morning, Jane harnessed the donkey herself and waited for Anne in the courtyard. She fussed with the cart as she fought to control her anxious thoughts. *Nerves*, she told herself sternly. *Just nerves.*

A flickering light caught her eye, and she glanced up to her bedchamber window. Cassandra held a candle in one hand and waved with the other. Jane knew her sister would pray fervently for them while they were gone. They had decided against telling Mamma about the trip. She was still unwell and remained in bed. If pressed, Cassandra would say that Jane had gone to check on Frank's young family, as he counted on them to do while he was at sea.

Crunching footsteps sounded on the gravel, and Anne appeared around the corner of the cottage. Like Jane, she carried a satchel, which would sit at their feet. The lightweight donkey cart was cramped, but they'd overtake the lumbering farm wagons with no trouble.

In silence, Jane walked the donkey through the village, down Winchester Road. The sun wasn't up yet, but maids and menservants would soon stir. Jane intended to escape the village without being seen.

Passing the last cottage in the village, Jane glanced at her companion. "I brought bread and cheese," she said. "Would you like some?"

"No, but thank you." Anne pressed her lips together. "I brought food too, but I'm not hungry." She peered down the road into the dark. "Are they nearby?"

"I believe so, and we'll be to the Four Marks turnoff in a quarter of an hour. I want to get close enough to see if they leave this main road to go help that farmer."

Ten minutes later, Jane caught sight of three wagons ahead and she pulled off to the side of the road. With the donkey cart half-hidden in underbrush, Jane and Anne watched. Not a man's head turned, and certainly no one turned a wagon when they came to the Four Marks road.

Jane glanced at Anne, eyebrows raised, but said nothing.

Anne ducked her head for a moment. "You were right. There's no barn raising."

"This is one time," Jane admitted, "that I would have been happy to be wrong."

The wagons rolled steadily on toward Southampton. The only changes were when drivers jumped down to walk and two walkers climbed up to ride. From Jane's veiled viewpoint through the trees, there appeared to be twenty or more men of all ages.

After another hour of trailing the wagons, Jane stopped for the donkey to crop some grass. Stretching in the morning sun, she removed her shawl and stuffed it into the satchel at her feet. They followed again, keeping their voices low and stopping when they got too close, all morning, all afternoon, and into the evening. A trip that normally took three hours had taken all day.

It was almost twilight when Southampton appeared in view. The setting sun left a pink-and-orange sky. Jane pulled back on the reins and brought the cart to a halt. It was wonderful to hear the sounds of the sea again. The repeated ebb and flow of the waves upon the shingle—the beach of small pebbles and stones—was something Jane had loved and still often missed. And yet, Jane knew, their errand today to the seaside was a sad and frightening one.

"Where does Frank's wife live?" Anne asked, pulling her shawl close around her.

Jane pointed to the right. "Down that road. Their house overlooks the shore. You can see the Isle of Wight from there. It's only a few miles away."

"Where do we go now?" Anne's voice sounded as small and tentative as a child's. "Toward Mary's house?"

"No, not yet." Jane gripped her hand and squeezed. Of course she was terrified. Her own family members were somewhere to the left, down on the long coastline of beaches, preparing to meet smugglers that night.

Jane kept a sharp eye out for the villagers while she talked. "Right below Mary's house, there's a stretch of high, fortified walls to help hold back the sea and any attacking ships. The stone walls are very stout, twenty feet tall, and eight feet wide. In other circumstances, we might have enjoyed a promenade along the seafront."

"With the walls there, how do you get up from the beach to Mary's house?"

"There are flights of steps built right into the wall in several places. When the tide is high, the sea washes in and out just feet from the great wall's base. You climb up the steps to Mary's house. It's called Rose Cottage in Castle Square; you can see over to the New Forest from there."

"I've never been to the sea," Anne said.

"I hope you get to come again in happier times," Jane said. "We lived with Mary and helped with her first children when Frank was at sea."

Jane and Anne looked out over the water, what they could see of it in the diminishing light.

"I had pictured the ocean much bigger," Anne said, sounding vaguely disappointed.

"That's actually the Solent, a strait only a mile wide in some places. That channel of water separates the Isle of Wight from our mainland."

Jane wondered if Anne was truly interested in Southampton and the sea or if her questions were to divert her own mind from what was surely coming.

Jane picked up the reins. "I think it's time." She turned the cart in the opposite direction from the town. "Further down are no seawalls, just the bare cliffs overlooking the water. Our Chawton men will be down there somewhere, away from the revenue men." She savored the salty breeze coming off the water. "We must go while it's still light enough to find them."

Ten minutes later, Jane spotted several Chawton wagons parked in deep sea grasses overlooking the cliffs. She stopped, a finger to her lips. She guided her donkey and cart around a corner, out of sight, then tied the donkey there. Jane and Anne crept forward and waited, hidden in the tall grass until the last wagon was unloaded. The goods were piled in half barrels and strapped to the men's backs. Jane recognized two of the men as the blacksmith and the cooper who had undoubtedly made the barrels. Weighed down, they followed a half-hidden trail through the weeds, then made a turn at the cliff's edge and disappeared. Jane waited several minutes, giving the men time to descend to the beach.

"Now," Jane said, grabbing Anne's hand.

They ran forward and lay facedown near the edge of the cliff. Jane heard muted voices below, but she could see no fires or lanterns. The last of the daylight would vanish soon. "We have to get down there now," Jane said. "We'll hide behind that group of boulders on the beach and watch from there." She stood in a half crouch. "Lift your skirts so you don't trip."

They picked their way down a narrow zigzagging track toward the group of boulders and away from the cliff where the men had carried—or dropped—goods for sale to the beach below. Hunched low, Jane and Anne stumbled through the pebbles to the nearest boulder and ducked down.

"Stay out of sight," Jane whispered, catching her breath. "If anyone spots me, I'll go forward, but you stay back here."

After removing her bonnet, Jane slowly raised her head just enough to peer between two large rocks. Voices traveled up the beach, but she couldn't make out the words over the slapping of the waves. She inched a bit closer. Her eyes grew accustomed to the near darkness, and she watched as several individuals—both men and women, she was stunned to realize—carried big, tarp-wrapped bundles out to the edge of the sea.

Then Jane gazed out over the water, and her heart nearly stopped. A large, sinister-looking boat, painted black with all-black sails, was anchored in the deepest part of the strait. Barely breathing, she watched as smaller black boats carried goods out and returned with bales wrapped in tarps, plus barrels and crates. Hefty men lugged the half barrels strapped to their backs, held over the shoulders with ropes. They stomped over to the cliff and began climbing while balancing the load on their backs.

Anne had peered around the base of the boulder and suddenly cried out. Jane dropped and yanked Anne back into hiding, her hand over Anne's mouth. Jane held her close and waited, but apparently no one had heard.

Jane whispered in her ear. "What happened?"

Anne wiped at the tears spilling down her cheeks. "I saw Papa. He and James are carrying a crate up the path we came down."

Jane was sorry she'd seen them, but thought that perhaps it was for the best. Now Jane would have an ally in the fight against the smuggling. Sooner or later, smugglers got caught. If only they could persuade the villagers to stop!

Jane continued to watch, but it was harder to make out individuals as dark-clad men and women trudged back and forth, up and down the rocky shingle beach, unloading the small boats. Jane searched for someone giving orders. Was Robert Lumb the mastermind arranging all this?

Then a man walked close to the shelter of the cliff. He stopped and struck a match. *Smoking a smuggled cigar, no doubt,* Jane thought. But then all thoughts were wiped from her mind as the brief match light revealed the man's face. Despite the longer hair and muttonchops, she recognized him.

It was John March, the young sailor from Chawton Village whose family believed him to be dead.

Without thinking, Jane erupted from behind the boulders and raced as fast as the large pebbles underfoot would allow over to where he was smoking. A whiff of cigar smoke reached Jane just as he spotted her. Anne arrived on her heels and grabbed Jane's hand.

"John March!" Jane said. "*You're* leading this? You're the person endangering our whole village?"

John puffed twice before bowing. "Miss Austen, as I recall. And I must correct you. I am the one *saving* your whole way of life."

"But . . . but you're dead," Anne said.

John March gave a bitter laugh. "I almost drowned, 'tis true. But when I washed up onshore down the coast, I decided to stay officially 'dead' instead of going back into service or being imprisoned for refusing to."

"You're a deserter then too?" The contempt was thick in Jane's voice.

John pointed the glowing tip of his cigar at her. "I hated fighting, on our side *and* theirs."

So, Jane thought, he *had* been a traitor and gone over to the other side, at least for a while. "But how did you come to be doing this?"

"We common seamen had a miserable existence, on English ships and American alike. So, I took my chance and escaped over the side. The sea washed me up, half-drowned, on British soil." He puffed on his cigar again. "I find I prefer smuggling. I learned about smugglers and pirates in the navy, and they were having all the fun and getting all the profit."

"Your mother doesn't know you're alive," Jane said, glancing at the group of villagers who had gathered around. "Or does she?"

"None of your business," John snarled. "Keep your nose out, if you know what's good for you."

"He's right." Robert Lumb spoke from the edge of the crowd. "You have no right meddling in our business. We're all surviving this war as best we can."

By illegal smuggling? Jane wanted to scream. But by the looks on the faces of the villagers surrounding her, John March wasn't the only one angry with her. For the first time, she was frightened of her neighbors.

How simple it would be for them to hide Anne and Jane

among the boulders or toss them into the sea or bury them in the shingle and never mention seeing them. Jane stepped back. The glint in Robert Lumb's eye said it would be easy and convenient vengeance.

16

Cabot Falls, Vermont
Present Day

*W*inter revisited Cabot Falls with a vengeance the next day. Sofia sighed as she maneuvered the freshly plowed streets after dropping off the kids at both schools. Mother Nature seemed to enjoy tantalizing them with a taste of spring before moving in with arctic temperatures and snow one last time before giving up her stranglehold on Vermont for one more year.

But the nasty weather made it a good morning to concentrate on the quilt research and use the computer before Jim and the kids tied it up all weekend. Marla hadn't sent her any genealogy reports yet, but there were still dozens of websites Sofia could explore. Wrapping herself in a Hudson's Bay point blanket to ward off the chill in the basement family room, she sipped hot tea and read. Time slipped by that morning as if Sofia were in a Jane Austen coma. If her stomach hadn't growled at one o'clock, she might not have returned to the twenty-first century.

By then she'd learned some fascinating facts through blogs, an interactive museum site, and emails with the curator at the Chawton House Library. Sofia occasionally got sidetracked, reading about Regency foods and how they were baked. The size of the giant open-hearth kitchen fireplaces astounded her. She laughed when she read, "The bakehouse was always separate from the house, and used for baking, washing clothing, and salting pigs." *How versatile.*

Unfortunately, while she learned much about Jane's quilting and fine embroidery, she didn't discover a single clue to help with Nonna's quilt. There was no hint anywhere of how her silk square could have been embroidered in England, yet end up in a quilt in Italy. Sofia reviewed her notes on the diary and painstakingly double-checked everything using her language translator. It all checked out, including that last line: *The quilt square disappeared in one place and reappeared in another.* But where? How? The diary left that part out.

Sofia went to fix a sandwich and make more tea, something with caffeine this time to jolt her drowsy brain cells awake. While she waited for the water to heat, she gazed at the dozens of photos and goofy family snapshots stuck to the fridge with magnets. *It's a work of art,* she thought with a smile.

Two photos caught her eye: a picture of Dad at his retirement next to a photo of his wedding day all those years ago to a young and beautiful Celeste. How odd to see her mother stay the same age Sofia remembered her, but see Dad age to his midsixties. Lois would never be another Mom, Sofia thought. *Never.*

And yet, to give Lois her due, Sofia admitted she was good for her dad. He got out more, exercised more, had more fun. And with Lois's historical work at PBS, they probably had some fascinating talks.

History! Why hadn't she thought of that before? Lois could well be a good source of information. She seemed to know a lot about England during Jane Austen's time, even if her know-it-all attitude rubbed Sofia the wrong way. Maybe if she took time to know her, she'd like her better. Before she could change her mind, Sofia picked up the phone and invited her for lunch the following Monday. There was probably more to the woman than met the eye.

Southampton, England
July 1812

While John March talked to Jane, his eyes constantly swept over the beach in both directions and to the cliffs above. No revenue officers had been spotted yet, but Jane knew from living in Southampton for three years that they patrolled twenty-four hours a day.

The Chawton villagers were carrying up the last cartons, barrels, and bales of something wrapped in oilskin. They dropped the bundles on the pebbles along with coils of rope, some thin as cords and some thicker than Jane's arm.

"You've smuggled in rope?" she asked, disbelieving.

Several men laughed, then quickly muffled their voices. John March grabbed a thin rope and waved it under Jane's nose.

"Ugh." She pushed it away. It wasn't rope. It was tobacco in disguise!

"Sometimes it comes as ropes," March said, "and sometimes in bales wrapped in oilskin. Watertight bales stay afloat for hours until they're picked up."

"But none of you own boats," Jane said. And yet she'd seen half a dozen make trips out to the black ship. It had weighed anchor now, however, and was moving silently and almost invisibly down the strait and back out to sea.

The end of March's cigar glowed bright orange. "Who needs a boat when there are other willing men with a sense of adventure?"

"You mean other men who are starving too," Robert Lumb growled.

"Who?" Jane asked.

Mr. Dowall stepped out of the shadows. "Fishermen here are starving without people who can afford to buy their fish and without safe waters to fish in." He shrugged. "It's not hard to find as many small English boats as you need to go out and meet a larger boat from the 'enemy,' as long as it all happens a few miles offshore."

Jane couldn't believe how astoundingly blind they all were. "Is any of this worth it if you're caught? You'll be hanged or deported halfway around the world or left to starve in prison instead."

John March grabbed her arm hard. "Keep your voice down." He ground out his cigar and then held up a hand for silence, and everyone froze. For a full minute, no sounds drifted down to them from above except the noise of someone climbing back down the narrow trail.

"Annie?" James Powell, Anne's brother, whispered as he joined the group. "What—?"

"Quiet," March commanded.

Anne kept her voice low and soft. "You and Papa are risking your lives—and ours—for brandy and tobacco. No one will starve without brandy and tobacco."

"Don't be stupid." John March waved a hand at the boxes at the bottom of the cliff still waiting to be hauled up. "We smuggle nearly everything that's taxed beyond what any person can afford. In those bundles you'd find tea and salt, leather and soap, chocolate and cigars." He grinned at Anne. "And French silk and lace."

Anne gasped. "My wedding dress?"

Mr. Powell stepped forward from the dark. "It's true, Anne. But you deserve a beautiful wedding."

John March gave him a shove. "Enough yammering. Get that load up to the road while it's still safe."

"No, wait," Jane said. "Please. I've seen your operation now, and I see who's involved. For your own good—for the safety of Chawton Village—I will report you. And if you're thinking of throwing me out to sea, you should know that my sister, Cassandra, knows where we are and why."

At that, John March chuckled low, but it sounded more sinister than amused. "Do you wonder how we know when a ship is waiting for us and why we've never been caught?"

Jane admittedly had no answer. "Who tells you? Some other traitor pretending to be dead?"

He lunged forward, as if intending to strike her, then stopped suddenly. By the pale moonlight, Jane watched an insolent smile slowly spread across his face.

"Some other traitor?" he asked. "Yes, I guess he is. It's your naval brother, Frank Austen."

Jane blinked, then swallowed hard. For a minute she was too stunned to speak. *No!* That wasn't possible. And yet . . . she'd never heard back from either of her brothers about how to stop the smuggling in Chawton. Was that why? *No!* She shook her head. She wouldn't even consider it.

"Frank would never do such a thing." Among his men, her brother Frank was known as "the officer who kneeled"—the one who ran a "praying" ship.

"It's how Frank provides his wife and children with some gifts—rather like the ones your mother has received. He lets me know when a smuggling vessel is due from France, and I see that his wife gets her fair share."

"I don't believe you," Jane said, but she noticed with a sick feeling that several of the villagers nodded in agreement.

"Like it or not, we're a team, me and Frank." March took another sweeping look up and down the beach, then overhead. "I'm what's called a 'lander.' I get enough muscle to get the goods out of the ship's hold and organize horses and carts for transport to a place of safety. Look around. You might know the villagers from Chawton, but there are people from other villages too."

Jane shuddered, and not from the damp breeze off the water.

This operation was so much bigger than a few smuggled bottles of brandy and material for a wedding dress. Even so, her favorite brother, Frank, would never be a party to this. Never.

"You're lying. No one in my family would knowingly be involved in something illegal."

Several men snorted softly.

"No one in your family would be part of a smuggling operation?" John March repeated.

"That's right. No one."

"Come this way." He took her upper arm in a steel grip and dragged her away from Anne and the others until they were across the beach at the edge of the lapping water where the half-moon reflected off the sea.

Jane's heart pounded so loudly that she thought he could surely hear it over the surging of the sea. *Will he drown me now?*

But at the water's edge, he abruptly turned her around and faced her west, toward the town of Southampton. "See where the seawall rises in the air?" He pointed. "See that house on the cliff right above the wall?"

"Mary's house." By moonlight, she easily pinpointed the house she'd lived in for three years.

"What do you see shining out of the window in the little attic, shining toward the sea but where no one in town can see it?"

Jane didn't answer. Her throat nearly closed up.

"That's our safe house," John March said. "The lantern that shows at sea but not to any revenuers patrolling the streets means it's safe to bring the goods ashore and up to Mary's house to store them overnight."

"I don't understand," Jane said. *And I don't think I want to.*

"Mary lights a lantern when the coast is clear. The spotsman on the smugglers' ship sees it, heads for the meeting place, and flashes a light toward shore when they're in place. Mary keeps the lantern burning if it's safe for us to come out of hiding and retrieve the goods. After we deliver them to her house, the men and women will sleep rough tonight, in wagons or caves. Tomorrow they'll go in groups of three or four, nothing to attract attention, get the smuggled goods from Mary's house, and be on their way. Some of them will trade or sell the goods in other towns along the way home."

Jane felt sick. His explanation and his assurance had a ring of truth to it. While Jane couldn't argue with the evidence that Mary was helping the smugglers, she still couldn't believe that Frank set it all up. He wouldn't.

John March leaned down close to Jane, and she shivered. "I'd think twice," he said, "about reporting anything you've seen. Snitches who interfere with smugglers sometimes find their cottages torched."

Jane recoiled at the threat and stumbled away from him. He headed inland, and Jane slowly followed. By the time she reached the cliffside, the moon was half-covered by clouds. All the goods had been transported to the top of the cliff, but Anne waited at the bottom, alone. Jane quickly filled her in about the lantern burning in Mary's attic.

"Does this change things?" Anne asked. "I mean, knowing Mary is involved and maybe even Frank?"

Jane knew she should say it didn't change a thing. She felt like a hypocrite as she wrestled with John March's words. If it were true about Frank, his illegal activities would get him court-martialed at the very least or imprisoned or shipped to Australia. Mary and the children would lose their provision, and the Austen women were not able to support them.

"We're going to see Mary first and hear her side. I won't accept the word of a traitor."

However, no matter what Mary said, Jane's goal of stopping

the smuggling ring had failed miserably. She couldn't halt it if the villagers were determined to risk their lives for it.

She'd read in the newspapers about various cottages mysteriously burning to the ground in the night. While she hadn't wanted to show fear to John March, Jane believed his threat.

17

Cabot Falls, Vermont
Present Day

Sofia kept her fear in check over the weekend. There were no more visits from the police. Was it normal to take this long to be served papers? She had no idea and was afraid to ask.

On Sunday afternoon, Sofia tried to put it out of her mind. She decided to make a fancy dessert for her lunch with Lois on Monday. For fun, Sofia created a cake that resembled whitework embroidery. She first frosted a round cake with a layer of buttercream frosting. She then used a tub of rolled fondant to cover the cake with a smooth, professional glaze. After it hardened, she filled a pastry bag with white icing and created the whitework design, copying Jane Austen's pattern of flowers and scallops.

When she finished, she stood back, tilting her head from side to side. It was beautiful, if she did say so herself.

And all the time she'd been working, she hadn't given Vanessa's situation or Julie's "get back to me today" message a single thought. She would deal with both after her lunch with Lois the next day.

Lois arrived promptly, filled with compliments about the house and Cabot Falls's quaint town square. They sat at the dining table, and Sofia found her surprisingly easy to talk to. She enjoyed hearing about her work at the TV station and her grown son in the military who was stationed in Germany.

"Wow, Germany," Sofia said as she cleared the table. "I'd love to live abroad for a while, visit England and learn about my heritage on Dad's side."

"Ah, yes, the Nelson ancestors," Lois said.

Sofia carried in the cake. She didn't want to divulge too much about the priceless quilt, so she chose her words carefully. "For fun, I patterned the cake decoration after some embroidery Jane Austen did."

"Well, it's certainly a work of art," Lois exclaimed. "Too pretty to eat."

"Ah, but that's what pictures are for." Sofia smiled and sliced into it. "I like to make the desserts pretty, but they're a failure if they don't also melt in your mouth."

"This certainly does," Lois said, closing her eyes after the first bite, savoring it. After finishing her slice in silence, she laid down her fork. "As I mentioned the other day when you dropped by, Jane Austen was a fine writer, but she didn't give an accurate account of what it was like for the average villager or farmer. Life was harder—much harder—than she portrayed. She also brushed over the realities of war, focusing on the bravery of the naval heroes but not the true conditions onboard the ships. England was at war with France and the United States while she was writing *Pride and Prejudice*, but you wouldn't know it."

"I'm not sure what you're saying," Sofia admitted. "Do you mean that studying the war conditions would help me find ancestors?"

"Maybe it won't, but remember that Jane Austen wrote fiction. You won't find your ancestors there. If you study the real daily lives of people back then besides studying needlework, you might find what you're looking for."

"Thank you. That's a good point. I'll try that." Sofia hoped she looked appreciative, but secretly she doubted the logic of taking her research in that unexpected—and unappealing—direction.

Southampton, England
July 1812

Heart pounding, Jane prayed for the quarter moon to stay visible until she and Anne made it to the top of the cliff. Constantly changing direction, Jane tripped twice while zigzagging up the hillside's weedy path in the dark.

Everyone had scattered and disappeared by the time they climbed over the edge, all but Anne's brother. When he was assured that they had a safe place for the night, he headed down the road and melted into the dark woods. Jane found and untied her sleepy donkey and led it onto the road, and they climbed into the cart. Her hands were scraped and bleeding from slipping on the rocks, so pulling on the reins was painful.

Anne's voice was faint. "Can you find Mary's house in the dark?"

"Yes, and there's a livery near Rose Cottage. We'll leave the donkey there."

The farther they moved away from the drama on the beach, the more Jane thought John March was bluffing. Mary, with her three young children, couldn't possibly be part of some smuggling ring. Frank would never allow her to do anything so dangerous. Anyway, couldn't the lantern in the attic be to send signals to naval ships and not smugglers?

After leaving the donkey and cart at the livery, Jane stopped down the street from Rose Cottage and studied Mary's house from the shadows.

Anne's voice was barely a whisper. "If your brother's wife is supplying safe storage for smugglers, where are they?"

Jane pointed at several uniformed soldiers patrolling up and down the street and seawall. "They're revenuers, on the lookout for ships doing illegal transporting. We won't see any smugglers while they're around." In fact, Mary would have extinguished her lantern as a warning *if* she was the contact John March had claimed. "Come on," Jane said. "I want to check something."

She turned around and headed in the direction of the gateway in God's House Tower, a section of Southampton's town walls that dated back to medieval times. From there they would have access to the Beach, a piece of land bordering the River Itchen.

"Where are we going?" Anne asked, a tremor in her voice. "Is this safe? I'd rather be up on the street, where the soldiers are patrolling."

"It won't take long," Jane said. "John March said Mary's lantern was a signal to them on the beach, a tip-off. I want to check it out." They slipped and slid over the shingle beach, the cobbles too big to make walking easy. Suddenly, Jane caught Anne's hand. "There," she said, pointing. "Up there. Mary's Rose Cottage."

"But I don't see any lantern light," Anne said.

"There isn't one lit." Jane stared, disheartened. "She must have extinguished the lantern when the patrollers came down her street. She'll light it again when the coast is clear."

"Don't assume that. Remember that John March is a traitor," Anne said. "How would he even know Mary lived there?"

"As a navy man, it wouldn't have been difficult for him to find Frank's address." Behind them, the waves rolled and splashed on the shingle, a soothing, rhythmic, nighttime lullaby. While it would have been more comfortable to walk on fine sand, Jane found the sound of waves hitting the pebbled beach calming. "Well, I have to find the truth, and we can't sleep on the beach," Jane said. "I hate to wake Mary up if she's retired for the night, but Frank must be told if she's involved in this."

Jane headed for the nearest set of steps built into the seawall. Its long shadow on the shingle blotted out the moonlight. As they neared the stairs, a bulky form dislodged itself from the darkness. Anne shrieked.

Jane smelled the rum on the scruffy man who plaintively held out his hand. "Move aside and let us pass," Jane commanded, her heart in her throat.

Mumbling something indistinguishable, the homeless man melted back into the shadows.

"Come on, and watch your step," Jane said.

Jane ascended each step slowly, vowing to herself never to climb a rock cliff or the seawall steps at night again, no matter how bright the moonlight might be.

At the top of the stone stairs, the strong wind whipped at their skirts so hard that it threatened to blow them off the wall. Bending into it, Jane led the way, glancing back to make sure Anne stayed close. The wall was a good eight feet wide. As long as they stayed away from the edge, the wind couldn't blow them over the twenty-foot drop.

When they reached Rose Cottage, Jane made her way through the garden overlooking the sea and around to the front door. The house was dark, but behind the gauzy curtain, Jane glimpsed the flickering glow of a candle. She knocked sharply once, waited, then knocked again.

The window curtain by the door twitched, and then the front door was flung open.

"Jane!" Mary Austen cried. She glanced at Anne and then back at Frank's sister. "What are you doing here? Are you . . . I mean, are the two of you . . . I'm so surprised to see you!"

Jane swept past, followed by Anne, and Mary closed the door. "Are you expecting someone else?" Jane asked. When Mary remained silent, she took a shot in the dark. "I was unsure about knocking. We noticed that your lantern in the attic had been snuffed out."

Mary's eyes shifted for an instant. "What do you mean?"

Mary was still an attractive woman, her pale green dress matching her eyes, but Jane didn't think she'd ever seen guilt written so plainly on a face. "We followed some smugglers from Chawton and watched them picking up contraband from a ship in the Solent. John March pointed to the lantern in your attic and said they stored goods here."

"Only temporarily," Mary defended herself. "It's gone within twenty-four hours."

Jane paced back and forth, up and down the small sitting room. "I can't believe this. Does Frank know?"

"No!" Mary reached out and grasped her arm. "And you mustn't tell him."

"Of course I'll tell him," Jane said. "How can you let him risk a court-martial by helping smugglers? How long have you been doing this?"

"Nearly a year," Mary admitted, shoulders slumping. "I don't smuggle anything though. I only wait for the flash from the ship's spotsman. When I see it, I light a lantern if it's safe but extinguish it when the revenuers patrol this area."

Jane sat finally and motioned for Anne to do so too. "Mary, you're signaling French traders while your husband's life is on the line, fighting the French. How can you do business with them?"

"I don't," Mary said, eyes brimming with tears. "I never talk to anyone except our own villagers and farmers." She twisted a square of linen in her lap.

"But why would you do this?"

"You know what the war's been like," Mary said, a pleading note in her voice. "The children have to do without so many things. But simply for lighting a lantern, I get free shoes for them and better food. I even have tea and chocolate now. Would you both like some?"

"No." Jane shook her head slowly. "I'm still shocked that women are involved in this illegal activity too."

Mary reached for a newspaper on a small table. "See here?" she asked, pointing to a list on the back page. "It says a dressmaker, a twine spinner, and a needlewoman were smuggling."

Jane snatched the newspaper and held it close to the candle. "It says they were caught along with dozens of others and punished in Lyme Regis Court. Is that what you want for yourself? What will happen to your babies if you go to prison?"

"I won't. I'm careful." The fear had left her face and had been replaced by defiance.

Jane suddenly was too weary to argue, to go on trying to save foolish people from their own actions. The confrontations on the beach with John March and the others, and now this . . . *Why can't I make them all see the dangers of what they are doing?*

A dizzy wave of exhaustion washed over Jane. She swayed, then grasped the edge of her chair. She knew Mary had nothing but baby beds, but she thought she could sleep on the Beach if she had to. "If we could make up pallets on the floor in a back room, we'd like to spend the night and leave very early in the morning."

"Of course you can stay." Mary hesitated. "You might hear knocking during the night, or voices. Don't come out."

"We won't."

"And Jane," Mary said, "you won't tell Frank, will you? His pay isn't stretching far enough, and often it is weeks late. We've nearly run out of food several times. I need to do this."

Without replying, Jane headed to the back room with Anne.

Despite her exhaustion, Jane slept little during the night. She only heard two sets of people at Mary's door, but she was too dispirited to care much. Despite the Lumbs' recent beatings, it was a risk they were willing to take.

But it was wrong. No matter what their reasons, it was wrong.

By sunup, Jane and Anne were ready to leave. They still had enough food for the journey, and Jane was eager to be on their way before the children were up. Before they left, Jane snatched the Lyme Regis newspaper. Maybe her brother in London could find out what had happened to the people arrested for smuggling. Perhaps a dose of reality about the consequences would shock the villagers—and her sister-in-law—into stopping their dangerous activity.

Jane paused outside in the early morning sun, reveling in the sparkling diamonds on the water and the rhythmic splashing of the waves on the beach below the cottage. The garden overlooking the sea was neglected, however. Jane saw no signs of the currants, gooseberry, and raspberry bushes she'd planted four years ago. Well, with three small children—and smuggling—Mary had her hands full.

After paying for the donkey's overnight keep, Jane and Anne wearily headed north on the shady Winchester Road. They'd barely gone a mile when they came upon a lumbering farm wagon with two men on the seat. Jane flicked the reins and moved to pass them, but one man jumped down into the road in front of them.

The burly man grabbed the donkey's harness. "Whoa, whoa there."

"Let go!" Jane snatched up the small whip in her lap.

"Jane!" Anne cried. "It's Mr. Gummer!"

Jane looked more closely, then laid the whip down. It *was* Richard Gummer, the miller from Chawton, with his grown son. Jane recalled how he had yelled at her to "Go home!" the night the Lumbs were beaten. She glanced at the back of his wagon where two crates and half a bale looked familiar. She hadn't noticed the Gummers at the beach the night before, but many had been carrying loads up the side of the cliffs in near darkness.

"What do you want, Mr. Gummer?" Jane asked.

"I won't speak of this ever again," he said. "I heard you on the beach last night. You mean well, but quitting the land smuggling isn't as easy as you think." He wiped a hand over his stubbly face. "I know, because we tried to quit."

"Don't tell me. You missed the brandy and cigars you'd grown accustomed to."

"No. And that isn't what stops many of the villagers from getting out."

He walked up to stand next to her, and Jane gripped the whip again.

"What stopped my boy and me is what stopped many of our neighbors from quitting. Farmers who changed their minds and refused to let the smugglers use their horses and wagons for transport and their barns for storing the goods were 'helped' back in line."

"Helped? How?"

"Our sheep would fall mysteriously sick. A hayrick might catch fire. Once, the pig jobber—you know James Ford?—was returning home late at night from trading his pigs and rode at top speed into a strong black cord stretched between two trees. Nearly cut his head off."

"Are you saying that's how John March gets the villagers to cooperate?" Jane asked, aghast.

"Not all of them. Some want to be part of it, but not everyone."

A light dawned. "You nailed the note to my door, didn't you?" Jane asked.

Mr. Gummer nodded and dipped his head then at both ladies. "I thought you should know."

Jane nodded, more horrified about the smuggling ring than before. It had never occurred to her that some of the villagers were being coerced into aiding the smugglers.

Driving on around the farm wagon, Jane pushed the donkey to a fast clip down Winchester Road for several miles. When Jane slowed down, she noticed Anne quickly wipe away tears.

Jane patted her hand. "I know. It just gets uglier. I don't know what to do now. If I report what's going on to the constable, it will mean prison or worse for the villagers who are being threatened into helping—as well as my own Mamma, Cassandra, and Mary. Mamma's health would not survive prison, and Mary's three small children would be left alone."

They got home in half the time by not having to stop and hide in the woods every few miles. By midday they were in Chawton, but Jane was no closer to knowing what to do. Instead of following an important lead, going to Southampton had been one big dead end.

18

Cabot Falls, Vermont
Present Day

After Lois left with a slice of cake for Sofia's dad, Sofia took her suggestion for a new lead to follow. She did a search for historical information on the "real" people of Jane Austen's era. It gave her a bit of a thrill to think that she could be related to the famous Nelson of such articles as "The Battle of Trafalgar—Britannia Rules the Waves as Nelson Defeats the French." Still, she knew the odds of being related to *that* Nelson were staggeringly slim.

While she didn't find the Napoleonic Wars all that interesting, Sofia enjoyed reading about the commoners' lives during that time. The wars dragged on for years. Lois was right; day-to-day life for the villagers was one of deprivation compared with Jane's lighthearted portrayal in *Pride and Prejudice*. While Jane rarely alluded to it, undoubtedly the Austens were constantly fearful for her two naval brothers fighting at sea.

Most shocking to Sofia was discovering how widespread smuggling had been. She'd always pictured smugglers like pirates—rough and violent, carrying knives in their teeth, and dealing in illegal drugs or slave trade. But in Jane's time, laborers and farmers from whole villages were involved in smuggling, trying to obtain basic necessities like food and coal. Had Chawton Village been such a village? She couldn't find any evidence of it. One thing that did surprise her was that Jane's brother Edward, the Squire of Chawton, actually owned the village.

But when she read where Jane Austen had lived before coming to Chawton Cottage, Sofia's breath quickened. She reread it slowly, not wanting to misunderstand. The website said Jane lived with her brother Frank's family for three years in Rose Cottage in the southern port city of Southampton. That was the town mentioned in the diary. What about the word *stowaway*? Could Jane have stowed away on a ship and gone to Italy?

If so, why?

And how far away was Southampton from Chawton Village anyway?

Could she find a reliable British map somewhere? *Ah, aerial maps on the Internet!* She could zero in on Chawton Village using the address of the museum. With just a few clicks of the mouse, Sofia zoomed in until she could see Jane's cottage. A building across the road was now called Cassandra's Tea Shop.

It was amazing to think that, thanks to technology, she was using a satellite image to see the British street that ran by the window where Jane wrote her famous books! The more she looked, though, the more confused she became. There was no Gosport-to-London Road going by her cottage, as she'd read in one of Jane's letters at the museum site. The Gosport Road was off to the east a bit, and it went north to London and south to the larger naval base and seaport called Portsmouth.

It didn't go to Southampton. Sofia sat back in disappointment. She'd made a wrong turn somewhere. What she saw on the map and what Nonna's diary said didn't add up.

Unless . . .

Sofia kept digging, trying to find an 1800s map that was comparable to the present-day map. After five or six map sites, Sofia finally found what she wanted. "Yes!" The discolored, wrinkled map was faded but still clear enough to read.

During Jane's life at Chawton, the Gosport Road did go right by the cottage, which had been an inn at a busy crossroads before Jane lived there. The Gosport Road was later moved when modern highways were built.

When Jane lived at Chawton, the turnpike crossroads was the meeting of two major roads: the Gosport Road going north to London and the Winchester Road going south to Southampton.

Chawton Village, England
July 1812

By the weekend after her trip to Southampton, Jane had decided to take the coach north to London as soon as possible to see her brother Henry. Mamma would not think the trip odd. He had acted as her literary agent before, and she was nearly ready to submit a final version of *Pride and Prejudice* to publishers now. While staying with him, she would get his advice about the village smuggling and how to protect the innocent from going down with the guilty.

Sitting at her tiny twelve-sided table in the dining parlor window, Jane copied the final chapter of her manuscript. A sudden uproar in the street made her drop her quill pen and spray ink across the page.

Murmuring about her own ineptitude, she pressed against the window and tried to see down the street. Something was happening around the curve on Winchester Road. Villagers up and down the lane hurried out of their cottages and joined a gathering crowd.

"Jane," Mamma called from the sitting room, "go and see what has happened. Oh, if only I were well enough to go myself!"

"I'll be right back," Jane said, grabbing her bonnet and lightest shawl. "Come with me, Cassandra."

"No," Mamma said plaintively from where she reclined on the sofa. "Cassandra must stay with me. You have no compassion for my poor nerves. Who knows what disaster has struck the village now?"

Jane hoped fervently that Mamma was wrong. They'd already lost so many sons, brothers, and fathers in the war. She dreaded seeing who had received horrible news this time.

And yet, as she stepped outside, the noise didn't sound like a reaction to bad news. It sounded more like a celebration. She would welcome some good news, some unexpected bright spot in the recent dark days.

When she rounded the curve, her heart stopped before her feet did, and then it beat like a trip-hammer. Standing in the middle of the lane, a head taller than the crying woman clinging to his arm, was John March.

Voices shouted from the crowd of villagers that continued to grow.

"What happened to you?"

"We thought you were dead!"

"John, tell us where you've been!"

Mrs. March, the woman who had been in wrenching pain in the posting station a few weeks ago, was now crying for joy. Her husband had died several years before, and until today, she'd believed she was alone in the world. And now her son was restored to her.

"It's a miracle!" she finally choked out, wiping her streaming eyes with her apron.

Jane edged closer. She didn't want to miss anything shared by the "resurrected" John March.

John held up a big hand, palm out, and waited for the excited crowd to quiet down. "No, I'm not dead, but it was uncertain for many weeks." He bent to kiss the top of his mother's head. "My ship lost a battle with an American ship, and I was captured."

His mother gasped. "A prisoner of war?"

"In a worthless hospital aboard their ship," he said, touching the side of his right leg. "I'd taken a bullet in the hip. The fever and infection nearly killed me. But when I could get up on crutches, they let me on deck to get some air. I waited until no one was close and jumped ship."

"Oh, John," his mother cried, "you could have drowned!"

"It was hard swimming with my injured leg," he admitted, "but I'd rather drown than be their prisoner." A grim look briefly passed over his face. "The third day floating in the ocean, I was ready to give up when some fishermen found me. I rested two weeks in their cottage before starting the long walk home." He pointed at Robert Lumb. "Then I ran into that good neighbor, who gave me a ride the rest of the way."

Jane's mouth gaped open at the web of lies. His heroic story was as fictitious as her own writings.

She glanced around the crowd. She recognized two men from the smugglers on the beach, and the threat on their faces was clear: *Keep quiet!* Other villagers shot her fearful glances.

"Will you go back to the navy?" one farmer called out.

John March shook his head, to his mother's obvious relief. "Here's why." He pushed through the crowd with a limp so pronounced that it was easy to see that his military days were over.

Only he didn't limp one bit on the beach, Jane remembered in disgust.

And she'd bet every bottle of smuggled brandy that by the end of the war, when it was safe to do so, his limp would miraculously heal.

Several village women followed John and his mother down the lane, calling him a hero, but Jane caught the eye of several farmers. Some had sons in the navy like Jane's two brothers, and the look of resentment—even hatred—was clear on their faces. For the traitor, John March, to pass himself off as a wounded hero was more than they could stomach.

And Jane knew exactly how they felt. Her own blood was close to the boiling point.

She turned back toward Chawton Cottage but then decided to check on Willie Lumb first. Having helped with his injuries, she had a special interest in the boy. She'd always liked him so much better than his father.

But when Mrs. Lumb took her to the tiny sitting room, Jane was dismayed at how ashen and listless Willie looked. "How's your arm?" she asked. "Is it healing?"

Willie nodded. "Doc says it will take time."

Jane caught Mrs. Lumb's eye from where she stood behind Willie's chair. She was clearly worried. The doctor's words— *lockjaw, gangrene*—crossed Jane's mind.

"Waiting is hard," Jane said. "Could I loan you a book? A naval book of my brothers', maybe?"

"Thank you. I like to whittle things, but I'm not much for reading," Willie admitted.

Jane expected that Willie had dropped out of school to earn money for the family, as many boys did. But look what that had gotten him: smuggling illegal goods, and getting beaten for his efforts.

Jane patted his uninjured arm and rose to go. "I'll get Eliza to make you some of her jam tarts to bring next time."

Willie grinned at that. "I don't have any trouble eating with only one hand."

"Very kind of you to come, Miss Austen," his mother said. "Did you hear? John March turned up alive and well. Such rejoicing for his mother."

"I heard," Jane said stiffly, trying not to let her feelings show. She was tying her bonnet strings on the way out the door when she ran headlong into Robert Lumb.

"What are you doing here?" he snarled.

Jane refused to let him see the fear that coursed through her from being near him again. "I was visiting your son," she said, "the boy you allowed to get beaten within an inch of his young life."

"Watch your mouth, if you know what's good for you."

She edged around him, then turned back when she was out of reach. "I was in the shop yesterday, and the shelves are as bare as before your trip to 'rebuild a barn.'"

"So? Goods sell off the shelves as fast as the shopkeeper gets them from suppliers."

"Not according to Mr. Watters. He said he hadn't had any tea in a week." She lowered her voice. "Yet I know it was in the contraband on the beach two days ago. I saw at least one bale."

"It was spoken for."

"An entire bale of tea already sold? I don't believe it."

"That's why women make poor businessmen." Robert laughed harshly. "You'd give it all to your neighbors. People in bigger towns and cities will pay higher prices."

"You let your own neighbors go without so you can make more money?"

"I didn't say *I* did. March runs the show."

"And doesn't he do a fine job, considering the war wound that left him crippled?" Jane said, sarcasm thick in her voice. "He should be in prison."

"Think twice before you do anything," Lumb said. "The innocent go down with a sinking ship right along with the guilty."

"I am well aware," Jane replied. *And the innocent have kept your ship afloat.*

That night, Jane's sleep was troubled. She tossed until her

sheets were twisted. A dream about bright, flickering lights woke her, but the bedchamber was dark. When she turned her head toward the window, she saw it was no dream. *Fire!*

"Cassandra! Wake up!" Jane flew to the window, yanked back the thin muslin drapes, and peered down, across the courtyard. Firelight was coming from the open door of the bakehouse.

Jane found her slippers and, with Cassandra following, felt her way down the dark, narrow stairs and out the back door. They raced together across the courtyard to the doorway of the bakehouse.

Jane couldn't see anyone inside, but a fire blazed on the ledge in front of the oven where all their bread was baked. Nothing burned on the other side of the room where the washing was done and an occasional pig was salted.

"Water!" Cassandra yelled, and they both ran outside to the well. Jane dropped the heavy wooden bucket into the well with a splash, then turned the crank to haul up the full bucket. She poured it into smaller buckets, which Cassandra used to throw the water on the fire. They repeated the process again and again until the fire was out.

Black cinders flecked the front of Jane's nightdress. Cassandra sat on the ground by the well, coughing. Jane got her a dipperful of water and then poked around in the bakehouse. What in the world had happened? Usually Eliza was so careful to push any live coals well back into the oven.

But then Jane noticed something odd. With a poker, she stirred through the black, gooey ash. The handles of a wicker basket plus one side of the wooden bread-making bowl appeared, scorched but only half-burned.

Their baking things were never left on the oven ledge like that. Someone had piled them up and set fire to them.

The words of Mr. Gummer, the miller who'd stopped her on the road, came back to Jane. While this wasn't a hayrick that had mysteriously caught fire, she knew it was a warning. Regardless of who set the fire, she was positive that the threat came directly from the ringleader of the smugglers—returning hero John March.

The threat had grown beyond what she could handle. Jane couldn't keep this danger to herself any longer. She would book passage on the stagecoach to London immediately.

19

Chawton Village, England
July 1812

Jane didn't realize she had dozed off until the London coach hit a pothole and jerked her awake. She must be nearly home to Chawton. A coach-and-six—a stagecoach with a six-horse team—made good time, churned up a good deal of dust, and delivered its travelers on schedule. When she was twenty, brother Frank had not allowed her to travel to London by stagecoach. At thirty-seven, she made her own decisions.

She stifled a yawn. London was always exciting, but it was a relief in the end to return to the country.

She stared out the window as she thought about her previous day. Henry's preliminary talks with Egerton, the publisher, were not hopeful. Egerton had only offered 110 pounds for her new manuscript. Jane planned to buy things for their cottage and share some of it with Mary in hopes that Mary would give up helping the smugglers. When the war ended—soon, she prayed God—normal trade could resume, eliminating the need to smuggle.

As she'd expected, Henry was aghast at the smuggling news. While he'd been well aware that it occurred down on the coast, he couldn't believe the people in Edward's village would do such a thing—and involve his own mother and sisters. He wanted Jane to hold off stirring things up any more until he talked to their brother Charles, whose ship was anchored a day's travel from London. As a navy man, Charles would undoubtedly know more about it than either Henry or Jane.

Late that afternoon, over tea and biscuits, Jane filled in Cassandra and Mamma about her trip. "Henry assures me that Lizzie and Mr. Darcy will sell very soon."

Cassandra frowned. "I wish you hadn't told him to settle for so little," she said. "Your work is worth much more than that."

That lifted Jane's tired spirits. Cassandra had always been her biggest supporter, in all parts of life. Jane agreed with her. Her new novel was worth more than 110 pounds, but she was satisfied that her brother had done his best. "Is there any other news?" she asked, reaching for another biscuit.

Mamma looked about to burst. "Molly Lumb came out of St. Nicholas's yesterday, sobbing so hard she didn't see me."

"Oh no." Jane felt a chill, as if a cold wind had blown past her heart. "I didn't think Willie appeared at all well this week. His color was almost gray."

"She wasn't crying about Willie," Mamma said, looking pleased to know something Jane didn't. "I asked what was troubling her. She said Robert had gone to Winchester the day before and had not returned. Mr. Powell drove to Winchester for her, but no one had seen him."

"Poor Molly," Cassandra murmured. "So many trials piled up on one another."

Jane stared out the window, her shoulders hunched. "Someone may have done more than beat him this time."

Cassandra's protest was interrupted by a knock at the front door. Eliza hurried from the kitchen, wiping her wet hands on her apron.

Before the Austen women could hide their darning and take up some fancy embroidery, the sitting room door flew open. Anne

Powell stumbled in, waving a piece of paper. She'd forgotten her bonnet, and tendrils of her blond hair blew in wisps around her pale face.

"Jane, look!" She burst into tears and threw her the paper.

Cassandra wrapped her arms around the crying girl and led her to a chair. "Eliza, tea," Cassandra called. Cassandra and Mamma looked at Jane, the same unspoken question on their faces: *What's wrong?*

"Anne, I'm so sorry," Jane said, kneeling down in front of the girl. She glanced at Cassandra. "The note says her fiancé, George Crawford, was wounded. It sounds serious."

"Where is he?" Cassandra whispered.

"His ship was in the Port of Genoa, protecting that Italian city. He's in a hospital in Genoa now."

"I have to get to him!" Anne cried, wiping her face with the handkerchief Mamma handed her. "I can nurse him better than anyone. And if he's going to die . . ." She nearly choked on the words. "If he dies, I want to see him first."

"You can't go there," Mamma said. "That's much too dangerous."

"If I'm by his side, we'll survive this together. I can't lose George." She took a deep breath and tried to steady herself. "Please help me."

Cassandra stared down at her own hands twisting in her lap. A tear splashed on her hand, then another one. "Help her, Jane," she said quietly. "She has time to see him, to say goodbye if she has to."

Jane knew Cassandra was remembering the death of her own fiancé in San Domingo fifteen years before. Cassandra couldn't see him when he was sick nor attend his funeral.

"If only someone had helped me," Cassandra whispered. "I know the pain she feels."

"Of course you do," Mamma said soothingly. "Jane understands. She'll help Anne get to her fiancé in time."

"Mamma," Jane protested, "don't make promises I can't keep."

Anne wiped her eyes. "I think I know how to get there, Jane, if you'll help me." She leaned forward and grabbed Jane's hand. "If we can smuggle goods to France, I could smuggle myself onto a ship to France. If I'm caught onboard, I'll pay for my passage with some of Papa's brandy and cigars. From France, I'll travel across land to Italy."

"Through battlefields? No, Anne, you can't." Jane gripped Anne's shoulders hard. "The smugglers are French. They're our enemy. You'd never be safe on a French ship."

"I don't care about safety," Anne protested. "I'd ride in a ship commanded by Satan himself if he'd take me to George."

Jane dropped her hands in defeat.

"I'm sorry for bursting in tonight," Anne said, "but I knew if anyone could help, it would be you. You know so much about the navy and the fighting. I just want to find George and nurse him. Marrying him is all I've ever wanted. This is my only chance to have my dream come true."

Anne, Cassandra, and Mamma stared at Jane, who felt the clear expectation—and the pressure—to think of a solution.

Jane stared, unseeing, out the sitting room window. "I *do* understand dreams," she said, thinking of her secret writing. "But smuggling yourself isn't the answer."

"Then what?"

Jane rifled through papers on a small table by the window until she found the copy of the *Hampshire Telegraph* she'd brought home from Southampton. "There are British naval ships in and out of Portsmouth all the time. Wives visit husbands onboard. I know that Mary's done that. I even read an article in this edition about stowaway wives."

Anne's face was so bright now that it seemed lit from within. "I could stow away."

"I don't know if you could or not," Jane admitted, "but being a stowaway on one of our own ships would be safer than on a French smuggling boat."

"Can we go right away?" Anne begged. "George may not have much time."

Jane stared out on the busy lane but saw nothing except pictures in her own mind of all the dangerous things that could happen to Anne on the boat or when crossing Europe on land. It was a foolish idea with little chance of success.

She turned back from the window. "You're determined to do this?"

Anne nodded, then ran to hug Jane. "Thank you from my heart. Can we leave for Portsmouth tomorrow?"

"We can leave tomorrow, but Portsmouth swarms with patrol officers since Her Majesty's Naval Base is located there. I'll take you to Southampton instead, to Mary's house again. She'll help you too. If anyone understands the fear for a loved one out on the seas, it's Mary." Jane rehearsed it in her mind. "Mary can put you on a boat to take you down the Solent strait to Portsmouth. She may even know someone willing to help you hide aboard a ship in Portsmouth." Jane gazed steadily into Anne's eyes. "I know this sounds romantic. But this is also a very dangerous thing you want to do. Do you understand that?"

"I do." Anne's lip quivered for an instant, and she pressed her lips together. "But I'm determined."

"Then I'll pick you up at first light tomorrow. Travel light because you'll have to carry everything you take with you, perhaps on foot when you arrive in France." Jane reached for her sewing basket. "And let me give you this now." She handed Anne the finished white silk-and-lace handkerchief, signed "With friendship" and her initials. "I most fervently hope you will be able to use it soon with George on your wedding day."

After Anne left, Jane and Cassandra sat up long after Mamma retired to her bedchamber. As Cassandra had comforted Anne, she now comforted Jane.

"I know it's dangerous, what Anne wants to do."

Jane nodded miserably. "She's likely to die before ever reaching George."

"Possibly," Cassandra said, "but after we've given advice and tried to rescue people from their apparently foolish choices, they may still decide to take the risk." She reached over and patted Jane's hand. "If they do, you must stand down and let them pay the price."

"I understand. I even accept it." Jane picked up the sputtering candle to go upstairs. "But I don't have to like it."

Very early the next morning, Anne was ready and waiting, a travel satchel in one hand and a basket in the other. "I hope to marry George, no matter how serious his wounds . . . I mean, before he . . ." She took a deep breath and squared her shoulders. "There wasn't room to pack my wedding dress, but for good luck, I packed your embroidered handkerchief. I want us to get married as soon as I find him," Anne said. "Then I'll live onboard ship, like your brother Charles's wife does."

Jane had no idea if a new seaman could have those privileges, but she said nothing. Anne would need all her hope—unfounded or not—for the days ahead. Jane had a horribly heavy fear that she was probably helping Anne head for disaster. But as Cassandra had advised, people needed to decide for themselves if they were willing to pay the price for a choice, and Jane needed to let them go.

Jane's cart had traveled only a few miles down Winchester Road when they spotted farmers removing tree stumps in a patch of former woods. With all the shipbuilding for the wars, there were fields full of stumps all over England. Jane recognized two men from Chawton. One was the miller, Mr. Gummer. Jane slowed, thankful for a God-given chance to try something Henry had suggested.

She stopped by an empty farm wagon. Mr. Gummer approached, his expression wary. "Yes?" he asked.

"I wondered if you could tell me something," Jane said.

"Maybe."

"You said when people tried to pull out of the smuggling ring, bad things happened to them. How many land smugglers from Chawton would you estimate want out but are afraid for their families or homes if they quit?"

Jane now fully understood their fear after the small fire in their own bakehouse. She knew it was a warning to back off, or the next time it would be the cottage. The bricks might not burn, but the inside rooms would go up in flames.

Mr. Gummer stared at his worn work boots, then looked up. "Maybe twenty people. Some families have only one person involved. Some, like yours"—he pointed at Anne—"have two."

At least fifteen families, Jane thought. Fifteen families whose father and breadwinner would go to prison or be hanged if caught. Fifteen families afraid to say no to John March.

She glanced at Anne, such a petite girl ready to take on a world at war, risking everything to find her fiancé. *Well*, she thought, *I can take a risk to help the villagers.*

"Mr. Gummer, please spread the word that there will be a meeting at Chawton Cottage tonight as soon as it is dark. It's for anyone who wants out of the smuggling. Tell people to go around to the courtyard and come in the back door." She picked up the reins again. "If we band together, we have the best chance of getting free."

Jane snapped the reins, and the donkey took off trotting. She pulled out the newspaper she'd wedged down behind the seat. "I'm returning this to Mary, but I read an article that might help you once you get stowed away. It's on the third or fourth page. I marked it."

Anne found it quickly and read aloud. "'There is a myth that war is an all-male affair and that women in combat zones, whatever their activities, are *civilians* and not *warriors*. This is confusing because, in practice, men and women under fire often do the same things. In naval warfare, everyone aboard—male or female, gunner, carpenter, or nurse—is truly in the same boat. When a ship is fired upon, everyone aboard is at war.'" Anne sat motionless and silent.

"Did you catch that?" Jane asked. "Nurses! They have nurses aboard. I should have known that. Doctors need nurses."

"But I'm not a nurse."

"When you nurse George back to full strength, you'll learn to be one."

Anne tilted her head and peered around the side of her bonnet. "You're saying that if I get caught on the way over, I can masquerade as a nurse?" Her tone was incredulous. "I know nothing about medicines or diseases."

"No, you could say you're a nurse's aide. You can clean and

do laundry and wash instruments for the doctors. There would be endless work for a willing pair of hands."

"I'm sure you're right," Anne said slowly. "I'll ask Mary how nurses on naval ships dress and try to look the part."

Jane and Anne arrived at Mary's by noon after leaving the donkey cart at the livery down the street.

Mary looked both surprised and suspicious at finding Jane on her doorstep again so soon. But once she heard about Anne's fiancé, her attitude was solicitous. "Come to the back garden; we'll have lunch there."

Over tea and bread and cheese, Anne shared her story.

"Of course you can stay here tonight, Anne." Tears filled Mary's eyes, and she cuddled her youngest child closer. "You received the message that naval wives everywhere dread. I know some families here. We can get you on a boat early tomorrow morning to take you down to Portsmouth. I'll try to find the name of a boat going from there to where you want to go."

"I can't thank you enough for helping me," Anne said, her eyes also brimming. "I don't know what I'd do without you and Jane."

Mary patted the fussy baby's back. "Jane and I have both seen how much Charles's wife benefits from living aboard ship with their children. I feel certain that if you can be with your fiancé, his chances of recovery will be much improved."

"I believe that too," Anne said, obviously thrilled that she'd found someone who so thoroughly understood her heart.

An hour later, after playing with all three energetic children, Jane brushed dirt and crumbs from her skirt and stood to leave. "I'm having a meeting at the cottage tonight," she said, watching Mary's reaction. "It's for any villager involved in the smuggling who wants out. Some have been pressured and threatened when they wanted to quit." She told Mary about the fire in the bakehouse. "I know it was a warning against my continued interference."

"I've been thinking about the dangers since you were here last time," Mary admitted. "I don't know—"

"Please consider what it would do to Frank's career and reputation—and your children—if you were caught." She adjusted her bonnet and grabbed her reticule. "I need to get the donkey cart and start for home so I arrive before dark."

Walking toward the livery, Jane turned and waved one last time. Anne and Mary stood in the doorway of Rose Cottage, arms around each other's waists. They would talk for hours that afternoon and evening. Mary would give Anne advice about being married to a sailor, advice that Jane could only imagine.

As Jane rounded the corner, she prayed fervently for Anne's safety, and that she wasn't seeing her for the last time.

Cabot Falls, Vermont
Present Day

Although Sofia felt her information on village smugglers during the Napoleonic Wars might prove important, she still wasn't seeing a connection between Jane Austen and Italy. Without it, she didn't see how the exquisite whitework quilt square could have been sewn by her.

But how could she find such a link? Who could help her?

Sofia finally requested a Skype call with a curator named Claire Spencer whom she'd been emailing at the Chawton House Museum.

At the appointed time, Sofia dialed and connected. After adjusting her webcam, she introduced herself and thanked the curator for her time. "As I said before," Sofia rushed on, "I'm wondering if there's any correspondence in your museum archives that connects Jane Austen to Italy."

Claire held up some typed sheets. "I did some digging after we emailed. I have a printed list and description here of what's in the archives. I may have found something. I didn't dig the letter out of storage, but I have the basic facts."

Sofia smiled at her very British accent. *I could listen to her all day,* she thought.

"What did it say?" Sofia asked.

"The letter on file is from Italy, written to Jane at Chawton in 1812. The person writing the letter, an Anne Powell, was thanking Jane. Apparently, Jane had helped her stow away aboard a ship bound for Europe."

"A stowaway!" Sofia exclaimed, then clapped a hand over her mouth. "Sorry."

The curator laughed. "You sound gobsmacked."

"I might be, although I'm not sure what that is."

"Gobsmacked? Um, you would say 'amazed.'"

Sofia laughed. "I see. Yes, hearing that Jane Austen helped a friend become a stowaway gobsmacked me, all right. It fits my research." *And a mysterious clue in the diary.*

Claire adjusted the computer screen. "Jane's friend Anne was smuggled aboard a navy ship at Southampton. She went looking for her fiancé in a hospital in Italy—Genoa, I believe—to nurse him back to health and then marry him."

"Do you know any more about her? Did she find her fiancé?"

"I don't know," the curator said. "There may be other letters from Italy, but it will take some time to find them. Not everything is catalogued in this list." She waved an arm behind her at the displays under glass. "We rotate Jane's manuscripts and personal correspondence. Only a small portion is on public display at any given time."

"I understand. But Anne Powell's name gives me something to go on." Sofia cleared her throat. "One last thing. I know this is a long shot, but do you know if the villagers of Chawton were engaged in smuggling during the wars?"

"Smuggling? Not that I've ever heard."

"But it wouldn't have been written about, would it?" Sofia asked, thinking aloud. "I mean, if they were doing something illegal to survive the war shortages, it's not something Jane would have put in a journal. She would have wanted to protect friends and family." Sofia could understand that. She felt exactly the same way about Vanessa.

"No, I don't suppose Jane would have documented her friends doing something illegal." The curator's voice had taken on a slightly frosty tone. "Would you like to be on our email list to be notified when we make changes in the museum?" she asked. "When we rotate the manuscripts and correspondence, we email our supporters and fans in case they want to see them."

"I can't come see them, but I'd love to know about them," Sofia said.

"I will keep looking for any more letters from Italy," Claire assured her. "I'll let you know if I find something. Cheers then."

Sofia sat motionless for a long time after disconnecting. She was on the verge of discovering the story behind the whitework patch. She knew it. But knowing that a friend of Jane's wrote to her from Italy wasn't enough. Not nearly. Was Sofia somehow connected to Jane Austen? Was her ancestor, by chance, this Anne Powell? She'd been the stowaway. Had the embroidery been a gift to her "in friendship" from Jane Austen?

Sofia would give Anne Powell's name to Marla to do her genealogical magic. If anyone could find the connection between that woman and Sofia's grandmother, it would be Marla.

Next, Sofia needed to give Marla and Julie her decision. She'd promised it by the end of the day. She hated to disappoint them. But, like Jane Austen, Sofia needed to follow her own dream.

Jane couldn't write gothic romances.

Anne Powell couldn't sit home while her wounded fiancé died in Europe.

And Sofia couldn't run a store with her painter friends.

Before Sofia lost the courage of her long-ago relation—whoever it turned out to be—she picked up the phone.

She phoned Marla first, figuring she'd start with the least intimidating friend. "Marla? I made my decision about the shop." She took a deep breath. "I don't think it's right for me at this time in my family's life."

"I can't say I'm surprised," Marla said. "I felt you were leaning that way." She chuckled. "Please, don't feel guilty. If it's the right decision for you, it's right."

Sofia visibly relaxed. "You know me so well. Thanks, Marla."

She dialed Julie's number next and repeated what she'd told Marla. "I'm really sorry," Sofia said. "I hope you find a third person to share the costs of running the shop."

"Is there anything at all we can do or say to make you change your mind?" Julie asked. "Your art and your desserts would be so perfect for the shop."

"I appreciate you saying that," Sofia said. "If you end up getting the shop, maybe I could join in with you at a later time."

"You'd always be welcome," Julie said. "Always."

Sofia felt sad but relieved. She'd no sooner hung up the phone than it rang again.

"Yes?" Sofia said, walking to the kitchen to start the vegetable manicotti for supper.

"Mrs. Parker? Officer Quimby."

The warmth drained out of Sofia at the chilled formality of Ryan's voice. "What can I do for you, Officer Quimby?"

"I wanted to let you know that our investigation is wrapping up." He cleared his throat. "I'm sorry, but tomorrow Vanessa will be formally served with papers charging her with negligent operation of a motor vehicle. We can come out to the house after school, or you can bring her into the station tomorrow."

Sofia collapsed onto the kitchen stool and had trouble catching her breath.

"Mrs. Parker?"

"We've been expecting this." She tried to keep the tremor out of her voice and failed. "We'll bring her in."

20

Chawton Village, England
July 1812

"Let's bring in a few more chairs," Jane said.

By eight o'clock that night, Jane was home, and she'd changed out of the dusty traveling dress she had worn to Southampton. The chairs that Thomas had moved into the dining parlor were full, and half a dozen men stood against the back wall. The drapes were closed, and the room was stuffy.

Jane was astonished at the numbers. She counted seventeen people, mostly men. She had hoped for perhaps five and had expected most of them to be women wanting their husbands to stop smuggling. She asked Mr. Gummer to come stand beside her. The room fell silent as she began.

"I know you feel, as I do," Jane said, "that meeting like this may be dangerous. I heard that some of you were threatened when you said you wanted to leave the smuggling ring. We, too, were punished with a small, unexplained fire in the night." She waited until the murmuring died down. "I'm not asking you to do anything tonight except consider what we have to say. John March is running the village and, unbeknownst to me, has been for months. Dealing with him on my own has proven dangerous, but I truly believe that working together, we can take back control of the village." She took a step back. "Mr. Gummer has a few words to say."

While no one in society would call Mr. Gummer eloquent, Jane thought he was splendid. He spoke from the heart in language the villagers understood. He was one of them in ways Jane couldn't be as "the squire's sister."

Even so, when he finished speaking and asked for responses, Jane felt the fear rise high in the room. At first, both men and women were reluctant to speak. But when they did, it grew loud as they argued. James Ford spoke for many of them when he said, "It's bad, I know, but going against March will cost us more than we're willing to pay."

Without warning, the front door opened, then closed with a click. Jane's heart raced. Who was out in the hall? Footsteps paused outside the dining parlor's closed door. The fear on the villagers' faces matched Cassandra's. Jane squared her shoulders to face John March.

The door opened an inch, paused, and then opened wide. It wasn't John March in the doorway. It was Molly Lumb and Willie, his broken arm in a sling.

Molly cleared her throat and looked slowly around the room. "I heard someone say that going against March would cost them more than they wanted to pay." She pulled her son close. "I say that if you don't get out, you'll pay far more. We paid the highest price. Robert's been missing for days, probably beaten to death this time. I nearly lost my son too. Only by the grace of God is his arm healing." She looked each woman in the eye. "I want my son out of the smuggling ring, and you don't want your sons in it either."

Willie leaned on the table with his good arm. "Listen to Miss Jane. She cares about you like she cared for me."

Cassandra helped Willie to a chair vacated by a farmer. Then she turned and surveyed the room. "Willie and Molly are right," she said. "Do listen to my sister, Jane. You'll never find a truer friend."

Chawton Village, England
November 1812

Four months after that pivotal meeting, Jane added a few more chunks of coal to the fire, thrilled to have the money to keep them warmer this winter. As soon as she'd received payment for *Pride and Prejudice,* she'd bought several things—including a new coat for Mamma—which made facing the winter much easier. She and Cassandra planned a trip to the shops with Mary and her children since Mary had agreed to forego the "extras" she'd enjoyed when aiding the smugglers. While brother Henry hadn't been able to negotiate nearly as much money for the sale of her manuscript as she'd hoped, Jane felt trading her copyright for family comforts was a good bargain.

Jane didn't kid herself. Smuggling had not been entirely eliminated from Chawton Village. However, at least fifteen people had stopped after banding together and refusing to bow any longer to John March. Threats had been made, and two thatched roofs had caught fire, but that was the extent of it when the villagers didn't back down.

And Willie Lumb—who now asked to be called William— had taken over as chief thatcher of the village. His arm had healed well, and he was nearly a man's full size. His father's body had never been found. But as the months slipped by, he was no longer talked about in whispers.

The squeaking door announced Cassandra's entrance into the dining parlor. "Wouldn't you prefer Thomas to oil those hinges? They positively screech."

"Never," Jane said, grinning. "There's no better warning for me that someone's coming so I can hide my writing and get out my sewing."

"Do you think you'll ever tell people about your books? *Sense and Sensibility* and *Pride and Prejudice* weren't just written 'by a Lady.' They were written by you."

"I'll never tell. Henry says I can't, that it's not considered a proper vocation for a lady."

Cassandra shook her head and rolled her eyes but said nothing else.

"I need to post a letter to Mary," Jane said. "Care to accompany me?"

"No, Mamma and I are endeavoring to teach Eliza how to make a Bakewell tart that doesn't taste like soggy sawdust." She shrugged. "At least the fire in the bakehouse is welcome in November."

"I'll return soon unless someone wants to share some gossip." *That is a welcome change in the last several months,* Jane thought. The village had once again become the friendly place she'd always treasured. People no longer avoided her. To the contrary, they sought her out to speak.

It seemed obvious now that their neighbors' coldness was predicated on the fact that the Austen women had not been part of the smuggling ring. Perhaps they had been jealous of the fact that the Austens hadn't needed to resort to nefarious acts to keep the wolf away from the door. Perhaps they were frightened that they might reveal any clue to the squire's family.

Jane put away her book of verse and straightened her music that was spread out on the pianoforte. Deep in pleasant thoughts, she reached for her heavy cloak and winter bonnet. When she opened the front door to step out, she bumped right into Mrs. Powell.

"Excuse me," Jane said. "How are—?"

She stopped, the shock on Mrs. Powell's face showing that tragedy had struck their household. She gripped an off-white envelope in her hand.

"Come in, Mrs. Powell. Please come in out of this wind."

"I must speak to you," she said. "I've received news."

Jane braced herself for sad news about Anne. Jane knew success had never been likely for a young woman searching for a wounded man during wartime. But Jane had held out hope, even as the months dragged by without word. She led Anne's mother to the sitting room and then hurried to the kitchen to bring her some sweet tea. Oh, Jane wished she could avoid this conversation. She didn't want to know for sure. She'd rather keep hoping. However, the look on Mrs. Powell's face confirmed her worst fears.

"I've had a letter from Anne," Mrs. Powell said. "She made it to Genoa and found George."

Jane was astounded. "That's excellent news. I had no idea." She poured the tea and handed a cup to Mrs. Powell. "I'm sorry, but you look so sad. What else . . . ?"

"Anne nursed George for nearly two months, but it went to gangrene. He died in a Genoa hospital. Anne plans to continue working in the hospital until the end of the war and then come home." She sipped her tea, blinking back tears. "She is devastated, but she's grateful that she found him in time. The two months she had with her fiancé were precious to her."

"So she never married George?"

"No. George wouldn't marry unless he knew he would live."

"I'm so sorry to hear this. Anne had such hopes of marrying and staying on with George to finish out the war."

"I need to get home," Mrs. Powell said, rising. "I knew you'd want to know. Thank you for helping her have that time with him." At the front door, she pulled her shawl more tightly around her plump figure and then stepped out onto the windy lane.

Chawton Village, England
December 1814

Jane sorted through the newspapers and post that Cassandra had piled on the table. One item was a letter addressed to "Miss Jane Austen." Jane recognized Anne Powell's handwriting. She paused before opening it and drew a deep breath.

Would there be more devastating news inside now, two years later?

Cabot Falls, Vermont
Present Day

Taking a deep breath, Sofia tried to absorb the devastating news. She didn't need to leave the house to pick up kids for another hour, but she grabbed her coat and purse the moment she hung up from Officer Quimby's call. Vanessa was being charged with a crime she hadn't committed.

Sofia didn't understand how her Suburban was seen at the hit-and-run site, but she believed one thing without hesitation: Vanessa hadn't been driving her car when it happened.

But how can I prove that? Time had run out, and she was no closer to an answer than the day the police officers had first come to their home.

Backing out of the drive, she glimpsed Pat Cooper in her rearview mirror, waving from her front porch. Sofia couldn't handle Pat's questions right then, no matter how well-meaning she was.

Sofia turned the car and drove aimlessly. Without consciously planning to, she ended up back at the theater, sitting in the parking lot, staring at nothing. Finally, she talked to herself aloud to calm the thoughts spinning like a whirlwind in her head.

"Now think," she said. "Timing. Timing." She stared through the streaky windshield. "Okay, the movie started at one ten. It wasn't over until three. Yet the police report said a car—*this* car—jumped a curb four blocks away at two forty-five."

Was that possible if someone had managed to "borrow" her car during that time? Could her car have been on Juniper Road at two forty-five but back at the theater within fifteen or twenty minutes, when the girls emerged from the movie? They would have come right out and headed back to school to be in time for the three-fifteen prom meeting.

Sofia drove from the theater to the house at 618 Juniper Road. Even staying under the speed limit, it only took six minutes to drive the quiet back streets. No one was outside. The weather was cold and blustery, the air damp and bone-chilling. Not a day to take your toddler for a wagon ride.

Sofia drove around the block on the way back to the theater to double-check the timing from that direction. Pulling up to a stop sign, she started and stared at the girl hunched over on the bench at the bus stop, a girl in a red coat with long blond hair.

What is Vanessa doing here? And is that a cigarette she is stamping out?

Sofia hit the brakes hard, and the girl looked up. Sofia immediately felt ridiculous. It wasn't Vanessa. In fact, it was the work-study girl who sold tickets at the theater, the nice girl who'd answered her questions a few days ago.

Sofia lowered the window on the passenger side and leaned over. "Hello again. Do you need a ride back to school?" she called. But the girl took one look at Sofia, jumped up, and raced down the street.

What in the world . . . ?

Sofia was stunned. The girl had looked terrified of her, but why?

The girl—Janeen, Sofia remembered now—suddenly cut across Maple Street, right into the path of oncoming traffic, where she tripped and fell. One car swerved around her and stopped.

Sofia jumped out of her car and sprinted toward the girl, who was sitting in a daze in the street. She grabbed Janeen under her arms, lifted her to her feet, and firmly guided her back to the sidewalk. Breathless, Sofia eased Janeen to the ground, then retrieved her backpack from where she'd dropped it. Crouching beside the girl, Sofia tried to shelter her from the wind. As she prayed for help and wisdom, Sofia realized why the girl had run.

"You thought I'd figured out that *you* took my car and nearly hit that little boy, didn't you?"

They sat in Sofia's Suburban, the heater running full blast, and talked. It took ten minutes for Janeen to stop shaking. "Tell me what happened that day," Sofia said softly. "Take your time."

Slowly, her story came out. In bits and pieces at first, and then in a sudden rush of sobbing words, Janeen relived the afternoon she'd nearly hit the little boy on the sidewalk.

It had been another cold, but sunny, Vermont day. She'd received a call at the theater from her mother during her afternoon work-study shift. She and her mom lived alone, and her mom had ulcers. When she called, she said she needed to go to the emergency room. "I was frantic," Janeen whispered. She had asked the usher to watch the lobby so she could leave for a bit. Her voice grew even softer. "I knew the bus would take too long, so I checked the cars in the parking lot. Yours was unlocked and the keys were in the ignition. I didn't even think. I got in and drove home." She was in a hurry and hit the curb, went up on the sidewalk, and flattened the trike. Anxious to help her mother, she kept going but checked the rearview mirror to make sure everyone was all right. When she got to her mother, a neighbor was helping, so she hurried back to return the Suburban before it was discovered missing.

"Did you lock the doors and leave the keys in the ignition?" Sofia asked.

"Well, I didn't want someone else to come along and actually steal your car."

Sofia sat in silence when she finished. Her heart ached for the girl, and yet she'd done something very wrong and had been willing to let Vanessa take the punishment for it. Or would she even know the police were charging Vanessa with a crime? Since Vanessa was a minor, it hadn't been in the paper.

Janeen's voice was small and hollow. She squeezed against the passenger door. "What's going to happen to me?" she asked.

"I don't know. I'll need to talk to your mother." Sofia thought for a moment. "I think I can safely say that my husband will agree not to press charges for you taking the car. I don't know what the little boy's mother will do. I could ask if she'd take your circumstances into account. She seemed like an understanding person when I talked to her."

"Thank you. I'm really sorry for any trouble I've caused."

If only you knew, Sofia thought. "Everything's going to be okay," she said.

By the time everyone was tucked in for the night, the whole mess had been straightened out. The police had Janeen's name and story, and Vanessa was cleared on the negligent driving charge.

"Coming to bed?" Jim asked, passing through the dining room with a handful of cookies.

Sofia nodded. "As soon as I send a thank-you email to the curator for the Skype call."

But first, Sofia opened an email from Marla. She had some results from her genealogy study. She'd found that Sofia had three Italian ancestors named Anne—Anne Righetti, Anna Lucente, and Anne Viscardi. None of them sounded British. "But I'll keep looking," her email promised.

It was ten days later when Sofia spotted the email she'd been hoping for. The subject line read, "Two New Letters on Display at Chawton House Museum."

Scanned copies of the letters were attached, but Sofia couldn't make out the faded, spidery script. Fortunately, the curator, Claire Spencer, had typed out the text of the letters written in 1812 and 1814 to Jane Austen from Anne Powell. Sofia read them eagerly.

The first letter said Anne had found her fiancé in a hospital in Genoa and nursed him for two months before he died. After getting some nursing training, she planned to stay on at the hospital to nurse others for the remainder of the war.

The second letter, sent a couple of years later, said Anne had married an Italian doctor, Salvatore Righetti, whom she had served alongside for over two years. *Righetti!* Sofia could barely breathe. Anne Powell, friend of Jane Austen, had become Anne Righetti, Sofia's ancestor.

Sofia eagerly read the second note: "For my wedding, I was married in a gray suit, not the white silk wedding gown I sewed back in Chawton. But I carried your white silk handkerchief in the ceremony." Anne went on to say that she planned to stay in Italy with her husband and baby girl. She'd packed away the handkerchief to hand down to her own daughter someday. "My life is here now," Anne wrote, "but I will never forget you, Jane."

Sofia sat back, hardly daring to believe it. Jane Austen had embroidered the quilt square in the wooden chest for her friend's wedding. That friend had traveled to Italy, married there, and stayed. And Jane's handkerchief had been handed down until it came into Sofia's possession.

"I will never forget you either," Sofia whispered. "Neither of you. Not ever."

Up to this point, we've been doing all the writing. Now it's *your* turn!

Tell us what you think about this book, the characters, the bad guy, or anything else you'd like to share with us about this series. We can't wait to hear from *you*!

Log on to give us your feedback at:
https://www.surveymonkey.com/r/SecretsOfTheQuilt

Annie's® FICTION